Mason Carr

Trevor the Time Traveler

Traveler

and the Murkian Threat

by

Professor H. L. Bray

ISBN-13: 978-1502772411
ISBN-10: 1502772418

Dedicated to

my wife Heidi and our five kids
William, Emily, Andrew,
Jonathan, and Caroline

who were my inspirations for writing this book.

Join the fun at https://www.facebook.com/TrevorTheTimeTraveler about Trevor's and Farrah's adventures, the science behind their stories, and when the next Trevor the Time Traveler book is coming out.

Special thanks go to John Eberle
for helping with the editing of this book.

Special thanks also go to the Fruit Smoothians
for protecting the Earth and the rest of the Milky Way galaxy
from invaders for billions of years.

In honor of the Fruit Smoothians, the chapters in this book are
numbered using their base seven numbering system which, when
translated, only uses the seven digits 0, 1, 2, 3, 4, 5, and 6.

Table of Contents

Chapter 1: The Time Machine

"Farrah, what are you doing in my bedroom?" asked Trevor, as he was waking up one morning. His sister Farrah smiled, as did the tiny rainbow colored unicorn standing next to her.

A bright light filled the room, blinding Trevor for a moment. "It was just a dream," said a voice inside his head. When Trevor regained his focus, the room was dark and empty, just like it was supposed to be. He was still very tired, so he rolled over and tried to go back to sleep.

"That was weird," thought Trevor to himself. Trevor was a little embarrassed by his dream, which seemed like a girl's dream. Farrah had been dressed like a fairy princess and the unicorn was super cute and had wings. He decided not to tell anyone about it.

Other than the occasional strange dream, Trevor was like most ten year old boys. He liked playing outside with the kids next door and mostly did what his parents and teachers asked him to do. His younger sister Farrah was nine and his younger brother Andrew was five and went by the nickname Roo. Trevor realized that since he was the oldest, it was his job to always be nice to them and to show them how to do things.

Trevor also liked exploring the woods where his grandparents lived. His grandparents lived on a hill next to a pond which had fish and frogs in it. Behind the pond was a small stream that Trevor could jump over, though sometimes his shoes got wet. Behind the stream was a vast forest of grass and trees with all kinds of animals in it like foxes and deer, and every once in a while a bear. But the most amazing thing Trevor found in these woods was not an animal at all.

As they had on many other Sunday afternoons, Trevor, Farrah, and Roo went on an adventure in the woods. They were careful not to go too far so that they wouldn't get lost. In fact, they always stayed together and close enough to home so that they could see their grandparents' house up on the hill.

Trevor's favorite show on television was about a professor who invented a time machine which could not only travel to any place in the universe, but also to any time. But the show was just a bunch of pretend stories, and he knew time machines didn't really exist. Still, Trevor wished he could have his own time machine.

"Someday, I am going to invent a time machine!" said Trevor.

Roo thought that was a great idea. "Cool! Can I go with you on your time machine?"

"Sure you can," said Trevor.

Farrah found this conversation very amusing. "Roo, time machines don't really exist. And Trevor doesn't have one, anyway."

"Oh, okay," said Roo, "but it sure would be cool if he did have one."

Just then, in the distance, a minivan suddenly appeared in the grassy field next to the woods. An old man with a beard and a cane got out of the minivan and waved his hands at them to come on over.

Chapter 2: Professor Sparks

Trevor, Farrah, and Roo were not sure what to do. Their parents told them not to talk to strangers, and they did not know who this old man was. It was also pretty weird to see someone in a minivan way out in the middle of the woods.

"Trevor, Farrah, and Roo, I know you are scared," called out the old man, "but you do not need to be scared of me. I am your friend."

Farrah yelled back, "No you're not. I've never seen you before in my life." With that, Farrah grabbed Roo by the hand and began to run home to her grandparents' house. "Come on Trevor, let's go!" yelled Farrah.

"I'll catch up," said Trevor. "I want to talk to that old man first. I promise to keep my distance."

Farrah and Roo ran home, leaving Trevor by himself. The old man waited for Farrah and Roo to be far enough away so that they could not hear what he said next. "Trevor," said the old man, "I have a gift for you." Trevor still didn't trust him, but he waited to hear more. "Trevor," the old man said, "I've come here today to give you my time machine."

Trevor didn't know what to think. Had this old man somehow been listening to their conversation? How did he know his name? And how did he know he wanted a time machine? Trevor couldn't think of what to say.

The old man, leaning on his cane, spoke again. "I made it my life's work to invent a time machine. I studied hard in school, especially in math and science. I learned as much as I could about the universe and how things work. Eventually, I became an inventor and a professor. You may call me Professor Sparks."

Trevor didn't want to be rude. "Nice to meet you, Professor Sparks."

"Finally, when I was eighty years old, I realized my dream of constructing a time machine. I've used it to travel throughout the universe, both into the future and into the past, and have had all kinds of adventures."

"Excuse me, sir," said Trevor. "Where is this time machine of yours, exactly?"

"Why, it's my minivan, of course," said Professor Sparks. "How do you think I got here?"

Chapter 3: Be Nice to Your Brothers and Sisters

"Always be nice to your brothers and sisters," said Professor Sparks, "and you will be rewarded with a lifetime of friendship and joy."

That seemed like another pretty weird thing for a stranger to say, thought Trevor. Still, he was pretty good at being nice to his brother Roo and his sister Farrah, so he nodded in agreement. But Trevor couldn't stop thinking about the time machine. "Can you prove to me that your time machine really works?"

"Sure. Keep your eyes on my minivan," said Professor Sparks, who was holding a remote control of some kind in his hand. He pushed the button, causing his minivan to disappear. "How is that for a magic trick? But don't worry. I'll bring it back in a minute."

"That is a pretty neat trick," said Trevor, who walked closer to the professor. "But even if I do believe that your minivan is some kind of time machine, why would you give it to me?"

"I know it's hard for you to understand, Trevor, but when you get to a certain age, you don't want to travel as much as you did when you were younger. Mostly you just want to spend time with your grandchildren. Time travel is better left to young people, people with a lot of energy and enthusiasm."

"I would love to have a time machine," said Trevor, who couldn't believe his good fortune. "But how did you know I wanted one? We were just talking about time machines."

Professor Sparks walked closer to Trevor. "A long time ago, when I was a boy, I had an older brother who was very nice to me. He taught me many things and helped me learn how to count, how to read, and how to dream. I always wanted to be like my big brother when I grew up. Like you, my brother liked time machines."

"In fact, one day we took a walk in this very place we are standing right now. My brother was talking about time machines and said that, someday, he would invent one. I thought that was the coolest thing I had ever heard. I was five years old then."

Trevor thought how weird it was to think of this old man as being only five years old, the same age as his little brother Roo.

"So I decided that I would go back in time and give my time machine to my big brother. He said that he would share his time machine with me …" Professor Sparks looked away, wiped his eye, but then smiled. "… so I am going to share my time machine with him."

Trevor couldn't believe it - Professor Sparks was Roo, all grown up. Roo had spent his life learning and studying so that, as an old man, he was able to invent a time machine, and had come back in time to give it to him.

Professor Sparks pushed the button on his remote control, causing the minivan time machine to reappear. "Care to join me for a ride, big brother?"

Chapter 4: Choose Your Own Destiny

"Well, if you really are Roo, why did you introduce yourself to me as Professor Sparks?"

"I have good reasons," said the old man, "but they are a bit complicated. To fully answer your question, I have to teach you a little bit about how time travel works."

"Whatever I need to learn to be a time traveler, I am willing to do," said Trevor. "But first, let me ask you a question to make sure you actually are Roo." Trevor thought for a second. "What is the name of my best friend?"

"Alex, and he has a brother named Aaron and a sister named Allie," said Professor Sparks. "They lived next door to us. We used to play outside together all the time."

Trevor was impressed. "I still can't believe it's you, Roo. How did you get to be so ... wrinkly?"

Professor Sparks laughed. "It happens to you too, Trevor. Remember, in the future I come from, you are even older than I am. Now, would you like to learn about time travel?"

Trevor nodded his head yes, but then asked another question. "You mean I am an old man too? Do I have kids and grandkids like you?"

"Yes, you do. But this is where time travel gets a bit tricky. In the future I come from, you got married, have kids, and many grandkids. But that does not affect your reality at all. You see, you still have free will. You still get to choose your own destiny."

"So," said Trevor, "if I make different choices in my life than I did in the reality you come from, then I will have a different life than the one you know?"

"Precisely," said Professor Sparks. "If you choose to never get married and have kids, then when you grow old you will not have any kids or grandkids. Your reality will be different from the one I just came from."

Trevor tried to understand how this could be possible. "So there is more than one possible future for me?"

"Absolutely, and this is the key idea," said Professor Sparks. "Imagine the entire universe, containing the whole world and all of the stars. This universe is like a single sheet on a bed with many sheets on it. People are like ants walking in the bed, stuck on the same sheet forever."

Trevor thought about this. "So there is more than one universe?"

"Indeed," said Professor Sparks. "There are infinitely many, all beautifully intertwined. We refer to this as the multiverse, which technically is a *non-Hausdorff spacetime*. The non-Hausdorffness of spacetime is what allows spacetime to branch into infinitely many universes."

"Whoa," said Trevor. "I'm going to have to google a few things when I get home!"

Professor Sparks smiled. "Excellent. Whenever you don't understand something, searching the internet is a great way to find answers. It's amazing what you can learn."

Professor Sparks continued. "Where was I? Oh, right, I was explaining how time travel works. You see, a time machine allows us to travel between nearby universes, like an ant moving from one sheet in the bed to another, and then to another, and so on."

"And when you move between sheets in the bed, that is, between universes, can you go to any point in time in the other universe?" asked Trevor.

"Pretty much," said Professor Sparks, "though this gets a bit technical. The main thing to remember is that you still have free will. You still get to choose your own destiny."

Chapter 5: Secrets

Trevor noticed that his head was starting to hurt from trying to understand how time travel works, but he was so excited he didn't care. "So, Roo, why did you introduce yourself to me as Professor Sparks?"

"Secrecy," said Professor Sparks. "I want you to promise me you will never tell Roo any of this. Let Roo follow the path he is already on. Let him become an inventor, like me. I've had a great life, one that suits me very well."

"Okay," said Trevor. "But shouldn't I share this technology with the government?"

"No, that's not a good idea either," said Professor Sparks. "In the time traveling community, it is generally regarded as irresponsible to unleash time traveling technology to the world at large."

"I see," said Trevor. "So, why me?"

Professor Sparks smiled, like he knew something he wasn't supposed to tell.

"You know something about my future, don't you!" said Trevor. "What happens? Do I do something great?"

"I have confidence in you," said Professor Sparks. "I'm sure you will do something great. Over the course of my life, you have been the most responsible and good-hearted person I have ever known, Trevor," said Professor Sparks. "I know you will use this time machine for noble reasons, and to make the universe a better place."

That seemed like a weird choice of words to Trevor. "I'll do my best," said Trevor. "And I'll make sure no one else finds out about my time machine."

Chapter 6: Joy Ride

"So how about that ride?" said Professor Sparks. "Where do you want to go first?"

"Don't you mean *when* do I want to go first?" said Trevor, with a smile. "I want to see everything."

"Alright, you asked for it. Get in." Professor Sparks opened the car door and, using his cane, slowly got into the driver's seat. Trevor just stood there watching. "Well, are you coming or not?"

Trevor ran around to the passenger's side, got into the minivan, and put on his seatbelt. "I just have to be home by dinner time," said Trevor.

"Trust me, that won't be a problem," said Professor Sparks. "That is one of the nice things about time machines."

The interior of Professor Sparks's minivan looked like an ordinary minivan, with cup holders and fold down seats in the back. "I find minivans to be incredibly practical," said Professor Sparks. "Also, nobody thinks twice when they see one."

It occurred to Trevor that maybe he had been tricked somehow, and that this was just an ordinary car. He had promised Farrah that he would keep his distance from this old man, and now he was getting into a car with him. Still, there was something very familiar about Professor Sparks, like family, which of course he was. "I can trust Roo," thought Trevor. "I'm sure I'll be fine."

Professor Sparks put on his seatbelt. "Don't want to get pulled over by a cop," he joked. Trevor smiled and relaxed a bit. "Jeeves, take us on the grand tour, the one of the universe since the beginning of time."

The car started humming, but in a very nice way, more like a powerful purring, like a kitten having a sweet dream. "What kind of engine does this thing have?" asked Trevor.

"It uses black hole technology," replied Professor Sparks. "It converts dark matter into pure energy. I know you wouldn't think it, but this engine has more power than the Sun." With that, the car rose gracefully into the sky and up through the atmosphere, like a rock falling to the ground from a great height, but going up instead of down.

"This thing is smooth," said Trevor. "No vibrations at all … and so quiet!"

"It should be," said Professor Sparks. "This minivan weighs more than all of the other cars on the planet combined. And its reinforced outer shell is so strong that we can pass through a star and come out the other side without a scratch on us."

"Wow," said Trevor. "That's impressive. Still, let's not do that."

Chapter 10: The Universe

The car was getting so high that the sky above was becoming a very dark blue, almost black. Trevor looked out the back window and saw the world racing away from him. When he looked forward again he saw the Sun rising over the Moon. The minivan raced by the Moon and then the Sun, like two gas stations on a road trip.

Next Trevor became aware of the vastness of space, and how great distances are between stars. Stars looked like dots of light whizzing by the minivan. After that, all of the stars seemed to be behind him, in numbers so great that each was like a grain of sand in a sandbox. "That collection of stars we just left is the Milky Way galaxy," said Professor Sparks. "Our Sun is one of the three hundred billion stars that you see, two thirds of the way out from the center."

Trevor nodded in appreciation of everything he was seeing. It was unlike anything he could have imagined.

"See that galaxy over there?" said Professor Sparks, "That's the Andromeda galaxy. In four billion years it's going to collide with the Milky Way galaxy. But don't worry. Our home galaxy will be fine. It will just get jumbled up a bit. Watch."

It was clear that the time machine was on some kind of preprogrammed course through space and time. While the time machine seemed to stop moving in space, the Milky Way and Andromeda galaxies started moving toward each other more and more quickly. When they hit each other, they combined into a new ball-shaped galaxy, like two flocks of birds coming together in the sky. "You see, no two stars actually hit each other when two galaxies collide," said Professor Sparks, "because the space between stars is so great. Makes for a great show, though!"

"Cool," said Trevor. "Where next?"

"In case you didn't realize it, we are now six billion years in the future. Now, we'll turn the clock backwards a bit."

"How much?" asked Trevor.

"All the way back," said the professor. "I am about to show you the beginning of time."

Chapter 11: The Beginning of Time

"Jeeves, turn the windows black," said Professor Sparks. "I don't want to spoil the surprise of what you are about to see."

"Who is Jeeves?" asked Trevor.

"Jeeves is the onboard computer who runs the time machine," said Professor Sparks. "Everything about this time machine is voice activated," he explained, "except when you are actually driving it like a minivan. That you have to do yourself."

"What do I say to Jeeves if I want to go home?" asked Trevor.

"Just tell Jeeves that you want to go home. It is as simple as that. Are you having a good time, or do you want to go home now."

"I can stay a little longer," said Trevor, "But I probably shouldn't stay out too much longer. I don't want my parents to worry about me."

Professor Sparks smiled and patted Trevor on the back. "I promise to have you home by supper. Jeeves, make the windows clear again." With that, the windows gradually became clear again, revealing a bright light outside of the time machine in every direction.

"Shortly after the beginning of time, most of the universe was light," said Professor Sparks, "bouncing around in every direction, like the inside of a star." He paused. "What you can't see is dark matter, which is invisible, starting to clump into huge blobs of mass that will eventually form galaxies."

"The same dark matter that this time machine runs on?" asked Trevor.

"Very good," said Professor Sparks. "You are a quick study, aren't you?"

Trevor thought it was both weird and funny that he was learning so much from his little brother, now a professor. But mostly he was proud that his little brother had turned out to be so smart.

The light outside got dimmer and dimmer until suddenly Trevor could see long distances in space again. Huge gas clouds were forming, spinning faster as they got smaller, and flattening into disks. "Those gas clouds will eventually become all of the galaxies in the universe. That one over there will combine with other gas clouds and eventually form the Milky Way galaxy, the spiral galaxy that is our home."

The time machine flew into the gas cloud. Stars were turning on like light bulbs all over the place. Some were exploding as well, sending a dust of many elements back into outer space. "When enough gas and dust collapse into a small space, stars are born," said Professor Sparks. "Look over there. See that light that just came on? That is our Sun being born."

"Those exploding stars are called supernovas," continued Professor Sparks. "Except for a little lithium and the gas elements hydrogen and helium created shortly after the beginning of the universe, all of the elements that make up our world were created inside stars that exploded billions of years ago, sending star dust everywhere. Some of that star dust eventually collapsed under the force of gravity to form the Earth. In fact, you and I are both made out of what was once star dust, long ago."

23

Chapter 12: The Earth

Trevor saw that there was still a lot of gas and dust circling the Sun. "You see that huge blob of gas over there?" said Professor Sparks. "That will eventually become the planet Jupiter. The other gas giant planets, Saturn, Uranus, and Neptune, are also mostly hydrogen and helium, along with other gases that give each a distinctive look and color. As more gas and dust fall into these blobs of gas they will get bigger and bigger, until eventually they form the four outer planets of our Solar System."

Trevor remembered from school that there were eight planets in the solar system. "What about the other four planets, Mercury, Venus, Earth, and Mars?" asked Trevor. He was very happy with himself that he could remember the order of the inner planets, starting with the closest to the Sun.

"Those planets, including our home planet, the Earth, are composed of heavier elements, like iron," explained Professor Sparks. "Iron is a metal which, when combined with other elements, is used to make strong and heavy things, like cars and airplanes. It is also what makes up much of the mass of the Earth, deep underground. See over there? That is the early Earth."

Trevor saw a planet of molten lava. Huge asteroids were crashing into the planet causing massive explosions. "That doesn't look like the Earth to me," said Trevor. "Also, it seems to be made out of lava, not iron. How come?"

"Lava is mostly burnt metals, like iron, combined with other elements, and heated to very high temperatures so that they have melted into liquids," explained Professor Sparks. "When that planet of molten lava cools down a bit, a hard rocky crust will form around the outside."

Trevor remembered from school that the Earth still has a liquid iron outer core, and that volcanoes are the result of liquid rock, called magma, making its way to the surface. He also remembered that once magma gets to the surface of the Earth and comes out of a volcano, it is called lava.

Trevor glanced back at the Earth and saw that the surface, now much cooler, had become solid. Clouds began to cover the Earth. Rains from the clouds gradually formed huge oceans. Continents were visible, and moved across the surface of the Earth.

"One of these times, I'll take you down to the surface to see some of the earliest life forms on the planet Earth, as well as some of the coolest animals, like dinosaurs. Just remember never to get out of the time machine. The Earth's atmosphere was not always breathable for us, and dinosaurs can be very dangerous."

Trevor nodded in agreement. "Are we almost home?" he asked.

Professor Sparks nodded his head yes. "Time travel can be a bit strenuous, can't it?"

"It sure can," said Trevor, "but this has been the best day of my life."

The time machine began to descend through the atmosphere of the Earth, through the clouds, and then back to the grassy field where it had all begun. Trevor looked at his watch, which said seven o'clock. "My mom is going to kill me!" said Trevor.

"Our mom," corrected the professor, who got a little emotional. "Please give her a big hug for me, okay?"

Chapter 13: Going Home

Trevor got out of the time machine and laid down on the ground with his arms out wide. He looked at the clouds in the sky and thought how happy he was to be home. "Time travel is even more exciting than I could have imagined!" said Trevor. "It's kind of scary, but I want to do it again!"

"I know what you mean," said Professor Sparks. "Without me around, I think it is best if you don't go too far back in the past or too far forward in the future. I've told Jeeves to keep it reasonable. Maybe sometime we can check out some dinosaurs together, though."

"Wait a second, where are you going?" asked Trevor. "I can't operate this time machine without you! I'm only ten!"

"Don't worry, Trevor, you have Jeeves. He can answer all of your questions as well as I can. I need to go home now. I've got grandkids to play with."

Trevor was stunned, but accepted this explanation. "Well, thank you so much for everything – teaching me so much, and the time machine!" Trevor gave the professor a big hug.

"You are very welcome, Trevor. But remember I am just repaying you for the many nice things you have done for me over the years. You were always a wonderful big brother."

With that, Professor Sparks started walking toward Trevor's grandparents' house. "Wait a second," said Trevor, "How are you going to get home?"

"I am home, Trevor. We are in your future, in my reality. I bought our grandparents' house. I live there now."

Trevor started laughing out loud. "You mean I am not even home yet!"

Professor Sparks waved goodbye to Trevor as he walked away. Trevor waved back. He was tempted to follow the professor to his house, but he knew he had to get home, and fast. He got back in the time machine, this time on the driver's side, and put on his seatbelt. "Home, Jeeves," he said.

Trevor thought about how much his family must be worrying about him. The last thing his sister had seen was a strange old man talking to Trevor out in the middle of the woods. His mom and dad were probably frantically looking for him right now. He felt really bad about this.

"Why aren't we going anywhere?" asked Trevor.

"You still haven't told me what *time* you want to return to your home," said Jeeves. "With a time machine, you have to specify *when* you want to get to the place you want to go."

"So can I go back to the grassy field, where my trip began, one second after I left?" asked Trevor.

"Will do," said Jeeves. As it had before, the time machine began humming with its beautiful sound. The brightness of everything outside the time machine dimmed and flickered like a fluorescent light, and then the humming stopped. "We are here," said Jeeves. "Be sure to take the remote control that Professor Sparks left for you. It is in the glove box. Just push the button when you need me."

"Thanks, Jeeves." Trevor got out of the car. He pushed the button on the remote control and the minivan disappeared. He pushed it again and again, and then it reappeared and then disappeared again. "Sweet! I can't believe I have my own time machine!"

Trevor took off running for home. Half way there, he caught up to his sister and brother, who were still on their way home. "What did that old man want?" asked Roo.

"Oh, nothing," said Trevor. "But Roo, did I ever tell you that you are amazing? Well you are. Don't ever forget it."

Chapter 14: School Day

The next morning, Trevor got ready for school like any other Monday. He got dressed, combed his hair, and brushed his teeth after breakfast. He put all of his schoolwork in his backpack and helped Roo with his backpack, too. Trevor got into his mom's car and put on his seatbelt, as did Farrah and Roo. But as Trevor did all of these usual things, he couldn't stop thinking about his time machine.

"Knock, knock," said Roo. Roo loved knock-knock jokes.

"Who's there?" said Farrah. Farrah was great at playing along with her brothers.

"Broccoli," said Roo.

"Broccoli, who?" replied Farrah.

"Broccoli doesn't have a last name, silly!" said Roo, giggling. He could barely stop from laughing out loud. He giggled some more.

"Okay, here's my joke," said Farrah to Trevor. "Will you remember me in a week?" Trevor said yes. "Will you remember me in a month?" asked Farrah. Trevor said yes again. "Will you remember me in a year?" Trevor said yes, yet again. "Knock, knock," said Farrah.

"Who's there?" asked Trevor.

"Hey, have you forgotten me already?" said Farrah, laughing. Everyone else laughed too.

Just then, their dad walked over to the car. "Have a great day at school, everyone. Learn as much as you can. Set a great example for the other kids." He always said this.

"Bye, Daddy! You have a great day too."

On the way to school, as Roo told another knock-knock joke, Trevor thought some more about his time machine. He thought about his trip through the universe to the beginning of time and back again. He thought about how he had met Roo, all grown up as an old man, with grandkids of his own. He wanted to tell someone about all of this, but remembered that he had promised to keep it all a secret, and for good reasons, though he had a hard time remembering what they were, exactly.

What should he do with his time machine? Should he go back in time to try to save the people of Pompeii from the erupting volcano, Mount Vesuvius? What about the billions of other people who have needed help throughout history? Is changing history even possible? Also, what about all of these other universes that Professor Sparks said made up the multiverse? If he wanted to save the people of Pompeii, wouldn't he have to do it infinitely many times, since there were infinitely many universes? It suddenly dawned on Trevor that if he was going to have any chance at understanding complex questions like these, he was going to have to take his studies at school very seriously.

"Trevor, you tell a knock-knock joke," said his mom.

Trevor thought a bit. "Okay. Knock, knock."

"Who's there?" said Farrah.

"Trevor."

"Trevor who?" replied Farrah.

"Trevor the Time Traveler," announced Trevor.

Farrah rolled her eyes. "That joke doesn't make any sense!"

Chapter 15: The Café Mobius

After Trevor got home from school, he went for a short walk outside, down his street and around a corner where there weren't any houses, just trees. He pushed the button on his remote control. His time machine, which looked like a minivan, appeared, parked inconspicuously on the street.

"Jeeves, take me to the future," said Trevor, as he buckled his seatbelt.

"When and where do you want to go?" asked Jeeves.

"Do you have any suggestions?" asked Trevor. With all of the time traveling Jeeves had done, Trevor figured it was smart to ask him for some advice.

"There is a restaurant that Professor Sparks likes to go to called the Café Mobius. Want to go there? It is ten thousand years in the future on the planet Allegro. It is a favorite hangout for many time travelers, which is why the professor says he likes to go there. It also claims to have the best gnocchi in the Milky Way galaxy."

"Sure, sounds good … wait a second!" Trevor was stunned. "There are other planets with life on them! What are they like? Are any of them dangerous? And what is gnocchi?"

"Yes, all intelligent life forms can be dangerous, but most of them are friendly, as long as you are nice to them … just like people on the planet Earth. Gnocchi is a pasta, like spaghetti, but soft and round instead of long and stringy. It can be quite delicious, I'm told."

Trevor laughed at the way Jeeves talked about aliens and food the same way, as if both were ordinary and commonplace. "Do most other planets have life on them?"

"Oh, no. Life is very rare in the universe. Most planets are either way too cold or way too hot to support life, or do not have the right chemical composition. That's why there are usually only several thousand different intelligent life forms in each galaxy."

"Several thousand!" exclaimed Trevor. "That's not rare at all!"

"It depends on how you look at it," said Jeeves. "Galaxies often have several hundred billion stars, and only one in one hundred million stars has intelligent life on a planet or a moon circling it. That's pretty rare. It's just that each galaxy has so many stars that, even at that rate, there end up being several thousand different intelligent life forms in each galaxy."

"Wow, thousands of different intelligent life forms! That's amazing!" said Trevor.

"Per galaxy," said Jeeves. "Since there are more than one hundred billion galaxies, there are probably more than one hundred trillion different kinds of intelligent life in the universe. Nobody knows exactly."

Trevor was speechless. He felt like Christopher Columbus discovering new peoples in the Americas, or like Galileo, looking through his telescope and seeing the moons of Jupiter for the first time.

"We are here, the Café Mobius. Say hi to Professor Sparks for me."

Trevor was so caught up in the conversation that he hadn't paid attention to the time machine traveling to the jungle planet Allegro. Outside the restaurant looked a lot like the rain forests on Earth – wet, and with trees everywhere. "How do you know he'll be here?"

"A few months ago, I brought the professor to this restaurant at this exact time. I figured you'd like to see him."

31

Chapter 16: Farrah's Disguise

As Trevor walked into the Café Mobius, he saw dozens of different kinds of aliens talking, laughing, and enjoying their meals. Trevor heard elegant music playing in the background and was intrigued by the aroma of delicious food everywhere.

Trevor saw Professor Sparks sitting at a table talking with a group of alien time travelers and walked up to him. "Professor Sparks, it's me, Trevor."

"Whoa! How did you get here?" exclaimed Professor Sparks. "Now I have seen everything! Let me guess … I must have given you my time machine?"

"Yep, you did. Thanks again for that!"

"You are very welcome. I've been thinking about doing that for some time now. Sit down. Let me introduce you to my friends." Trevor sat down at the table and smiled at the two aliens seated across from him.

"First of all, put on this earpiece," said Professor Sparks. "It translates everyone's words into English for you."

Trevor inserted the device into his ear. "My name is Banana Splash," said the first alien, who kind of looked like a bear in the face, but like humans only had hair on his head. "Nice to meet you. Want to hear a knock-knock joke?"

Trevor thought for a second and realized that Roo, even as Professor Sparks, was still spreading his brand of humor throughout the universe.

"That's okay," said Trevor. "I think I know all of the professor's jokes already. Is your name really Banana Splash, or is my translator not working correctly?"

Professor Sparks explained, "The translator in your ear translates names to something recognizable to you in our language. To help you remember where people are from, each planet is given its own theme. For example, people from Banana Splash's planet are assigned names related to food. People from this planet, the planet Allegro, are assigned names related to music. Banana Splash's real name is something that we couldn't even pronounce. Banana, as I like to call him, is a great guy. A lot of fun at parties, too."

Trevor shook Banana's hand, which had seven fingers on it. "Nice to meet you, Banana Splash." Trevor then extended his hand to the other alien at the table, who looked kind of like an octopus, with tentacles for arms. "Hi, I'm Trevor."

"Yes, I know who you are," said the other alien. "Actually, I've known you your whole life." With that, the alien changed into human form, and suddenly looked like Farrah, Trevor's sister. "Hi, Trevor!"

"Farrah, is that you? What are you doing here?" Trevor was very surprised.

"Of course it's me, silly. You gave me a ride here!"

Chapter 20: Banana Splash

"Sorry for the deception, Professor Sparks," said Farrah, who had been in disguise. "Trevor wasn't sure if you'd be mad that he let me come along with him on his time travels. We still didn't tell Roo, though, as you requested."

"Quite alright," said Professor Sparks. "I like surprises!"

"But I didn't bring you with me," said Trevor. "I came here by myself."

"I'm not talking about you, Trevor," said Farrah. "I'm talking about the other Trevor, over there!" Farrah pointed at another alien sitting at another table who, at Farrah's request, turned into human form, becoming another Trevor. The other Trevor got up and walked over.

"Hi, everyone!" said the other Trevor. "Be sure to try the gnocchi here, it's delicious! I'd love to stick around and talk with all of you, but I think I'm going to head back home now. I'm getting pretty tired. Hey Professor. Hi Trevor. Good to see both of you again. Farrah, are you ready to go?"

"I'm going to hang out here some more, if you don't mind," said Farrah. "I'll catch a ride home with someone else." With that, the other Trevor waved goodbye and walked out the door.

Trevor's head was spinning as he waved goodbye to himself. "This place is awesome!" said Trevor.

"I see. This must be your first time here?" said Farrah. "Well, stick with Professor Sparks and me. We'll show you around."

"Who was that other Trevor?" asked Trevor. "Was that me, from the future?"

"Not necessarily," explained the professor. "It might be you in the future, depending on the choices you make. Or it might not be you. All we know is that one of the Trevors from one of your realities decided to give Farrah a lift here."

Banana Splash was enjoying the confused look on Trevor's face. "You guys are fun!" he said. "Listen, Trevor, you can either spend your whole life trying to understand time travel like the professor here, or you can just go with it. Myself, I just go with it. You guys want to have some fun?"

"Sure," said Trevor.

Professor Sparks and Farrah seemed interested too, but Professor Sparks looked suspicious. "What do you have in mind, exactly?"

"It's a surprise. Meet me out front in Trevor's time machine in one minute. I've got to say goodbye to some friends before I leave."

With that, Trevor, Farrah, and Professor Sparks got up from their table, waved goodbye to a couple of friends, and then made their way to Trevor's time machine. "Shotgun!" said Farrah, which was her way of claiming the seat next to Trevor in the front row of the minivan.

Professor Sparks laughed. "I guess I'll take the backseat. Funny how things never change! At least this minivan has a sliding door. Makes it easier for an old man like me."

As the three siblings from different realities buckled up in the minivan, Banana Splash ran out of the restaurant carrying a bag and dove head first into Trevor's time machine. "Hit it!" said Banana Splash. "They're after me!"

Chapter 21: Escape

Three particularly ugly and angry looking aliens came running out of the restaurant looking for Banana Splash. They pointed at Trevor's time machine and started running toward it.

"Jeeves," said Trevor, "get us out of here!" Jeeves then asked for specifics about when and where he wanted to go. "I don't know, anywhere!" said Trevor.

"Banana time out!" yelled Banana Splash.

With that, everything outside Trevor's time machine became frozen in time. The three angry aliens were frozen, as was the drool coming out of their mouths. The music and smells coming from the restaurant were gone too. Everything was completely silent.

"What did you do?" asked Trevor.

"Oh, I called a banana time out," said Banana Splash. "I was born with the ability to freeze time. I wanted to have a chance to explain to you all why I stole the bag belonging to those three angry aliens."

"Okay, explain away," said Professor Sparks. "I am sure this will be good."

"Well, muffle puffle swiffle bubbles. Also, baffle twaffle twiddle riddle, and happy lappy puppy wuppy." Banana Splash looked straight at everyone and smiled.

"I don't think the translator in my ear is working correctly," said Trevor. "All I am hearing is gibberish … and something about puppies?"

"No, your translator is working just fine," said Professor Sparks. "Banana is making fun of us, I think."

"Look, I can't explain it in terms you would understand, but I know those guys were up to something bad. I know when something isn't right, and trust me, those guys aren't right." Banana Splash walked over to the three angry aliens. "Also, look at their faces. These guys aren't coming over here to get their bag back. They're coming over here to hurt us. Whatever they're up to, we need to stop them."

Farrah nodded in agreement. "Let's do it! Let's stop those guys from whatever bad stuff they were going to do!" She looked over to Professor Sparks to see what he thought.

Professor Sparks stroked his beard with purpose, as if it helped him think hard and deeply. "Well, I don't condone theft, Banana, but I think you might be right. That is only because you have always been right in the past. But you must promise me that if we find out that they were not doing anything wrong, then you will return their bag to them and apologize most sincerely."

"Done," said Banana Splash, who ran back inside the restaurant and came out with three ice cream cones. He put one ice cream cone in the pants of each of the three angry frozen aliens. "I can apologize for that, too."

Professor Sparks sighed. "Get in the car, you trouble maker, before you go too far!"

As the time machine was leaving the restaurant, Banana Splash yelled out the window, "Banana time in!" The angry aliens leapt for the time machine, only to miss it and form a pile on the ground.

"We'll get you" they yelled, as they shook their fists, "if it's the last thing we do!"

Chapter 22: Too Close

Trevor, Farrah, Professor Sparks, and Banana Splash looked at each other for a moment, and then started laughing out loud. "You *are* crazy!" said Trevor to Banana Splash.

"And I haven't even told you the best part!" snorted Banana Splash, who was laughing so hard he could barely talk. "I implanted a tracking device in each of those aliens! The ice cream is just to keep the swelling down!"

Farrah, who was finishing off some kind of milk-like drink from the restaurant, laughed so hard that some of her drink came out of her nose. "You what?" she exclaimed, with tears in her eyes. "That's disgusting!" As she laughed, only her seatbelt stopped her from falling onto the floor of the minivan.

Professor Sparks, who was also clearly amused, tried to be the responsible one in the group. "Okay, let's have a look in this bag that you stole."

Banana Splash reached into the bag and pulled out an electronic device the size of a shoe box with wires everywhere and a timer that was counting down. "25, 24, 23, 22 ..."

"It's a bomb!" yelled Trevor. "Quick, throw it out the window!"

"19, 18, 17, 16 ..." read the timer on the device.

"We can't roll down the windows," said Professor Sparks, "We're in outer space! Jeeves, take us somewhere with a breathable atmosphere, and fast!" Jeeves changed course and raced toward a planet in the distance.

"13, 12, 11, 10 ..." read the timer, as the minivan approached the outer atmosphere of the planet.

"We're not going to make it!" yelled Trevor. "Can't you call a banana time out?"

"7, 6, 5, 4 ..." Everyone braced for an explosion.

"Oh, yeah, I can. Banana time out!" yelled Banana Splash. The timer stopped ticking at 3. "I put a banana time out field around the bomb," said Banana Splash. "We're perfectly safe now."

Everyone looked at each other again, but now no one was laughing. "Well, one thing is for sure," said Professor Sparks, "Those guys *were* up to no good. If Banana hadn't done what he did, there is no telling how many people in that restaurant might be dead right now."

Chapter 23: Courage

Trevor, Farrah, Professor Sparks, and Banana Splash landed their time machine on the planet's surface. "Where are we?" asked Trevor. He looked around at a barren landscape of deserts and mountains and saw a green planet nearby on the horizon.

"We're actually on a moon that circles the planet Allegro," said Jeeves. "No one lives here because there is not enough water to support life." Everyone got out of the time machine to stretch their legs a bit.

"We could have been killed!" yelled Farrah. Her near death experience with the bomb was starting to sink in. "I want to go home."

"Yes, I think that is a good idea," said Professor Sparks. "This kind of adventure is much too dangerous for children. Trevor, I think you should go home too."

"I thought you guys wanted to have fun!" joked Banana Splash. "Wasn't that the most exciting experience of your life? We saved all those people too, which is pretty cool."

Trevor had to admit he was having fun. "But what are we going to do if those angry aliens come after us? We're completely defenseless."

Banana Splash thought for a second. "What if I could give you the means to defend yourselves? Would you help me stop those bad guys then?"

Trevor and Farrah nodded in agreement. "What do you mean, exactly?" asked Trevor.

"Come with me to my home planet, which is a place of much beauty. I have many friends there who can help us, and we can get some rest. After that, some friends of mine will teach you how to defend yourselves, no matter what the situation."

Trevor and Farrah were both curious. "You mean like karate lessons?" asked Trevor.

"Sure, like karate lessons," said Banana Splash. "Let's just say that no one will ever push you around again."

"Well, I'm in," said Professor Sparks. "I know a good cause when I see one. But whether or not you children want to go on this adventure is entirely up to you."

Trevor thought for a second. "What do you think we should do, Professor Sparks?"

"Well, you helped save many lives at the Café Mobius, so you are already heroes. You can go home now and feel very good about yourselves. But ignoring evil does not make it go away, and good people need all the help they can get. Banana is giving you this chance, the chance to do even more good in the universe. The decision is yours."

"I want to help," said Farrah, "but I'm still scared." Trevor was a bit unnerved, too.

"Courage," said Professor Sparks, "is doing what is right, even when you are scared."

Trevor and Farrah looked at each other, thought for a minute, and then read each other's face. Their serious faces became more relaxed, but focused. "We're in," said Trevor. "Teach us what we need to know."

Chapter 24: Fruit Smoothie

"Jeeves, take us to Banana's home planet, the planet …
Banana, what is your planet called?" asked Trevor.

"Fruit Smoothie," said Banana Splash.

"… the planet Fruit Smoothie," said Trevor, who couldn't help
but start chuckling and smiling broadly. Farrah did too. "Sorry, the
names from your planet translate to funny words for us," said
Trevor. "No disrespect intended." Banana smiled back.

The time machine made its way through interstellar space and
approached a blue-green planet that resembled the Earth. "Fruit
Smoothie has been a peaceful planet for billions of years," said
Banana Splash, "allowing us to become one of the wealthiest
societies in the galaxy. We are also all experts at a form of self-
defense we call Juicy Juicy."

"Will you teach us Juicy Juicy?" asked Farrah.

Banana nodded his head yes as he gave directions to Jeeves on
where to land. "Please, come to my home. You are my honored
guests."

Trevor, Farrah, and Professor Sparks followed Banana Splash into his home and left the time machine in his backyard. The first room they entered had an indoor pool in it, along with a sauna and a steam room. "Pretty fancy," said Professor Sparks.

Banana Splash then asked them all of stand in a row, next to the pool. "On my planet, it is traditional to close your eyes and meditate for a moment when you enter someone's house, all while standing on one foot." They closed their eyes and stood on one foot. Banana then pushed all of them into the pool and started laughing.

"Those are your first two lessons in Juicy Juicy. First, if you want someone to do something, try asking nicely. Second, never stand next to a pool on one foot with your eyes closed."

Professor Sparks did not seem amused. "I am too old for practical jokes of this nature!" said the professor. "I can barely walk without a cane, and I have no idea how I am going to get out of this pool. Would you please give me a hand?"

Banana Splash leaned over to help the professor out of the pool. The professor grabbed Banana's hand and held on hard. "Trevor, Farrah, let's give Banana a dose of his own medicine!" Trevor and Farrah grabbed Banana by the wrist and helped the professor pull Banana Splash into the pool too.

Banana Splash fell into the pool head first with a big splash, and then stood up, wiping the water from his face. He smiled at his students, as if proud of what a great teacher he was. "Well done," said Banana, "Well done!"

Chapter 25: Dinner Time

Trevor, Farrah, Professor Sparks, and Banana Splash enjoyed splashing around in the pool. "Well, I've got to go home now," said Trevor. "I need some dry clothes, and I'm getting pretty hungry." His watch, which fortunately was waterproof, read six o'clock.

"Don't be silly," said Banana Splash. "You are my guests." With that, Banana made a gesture with his hand which caused all of the water in the pool to disappear. Everyone was perfectly dry and standing in an empty pool.

"Whoa, that was amazing!" said Farrah. Banana then made another gesture with his hand which transformed the room into an elegant dining room. Everyone was now seated at a beautifully decorated dinner table set for four. "And that was even more amazing!" said Farrah.

A round plate and an empty glass were in front of each person. "Just think of any food and drink that you like, and it will appear before you," said Banana Splash.

Trevor wished for pepperoni pizza, carrot sticks, and mashed potatoes and gravy, all of which appeared on his plate. He then wished for some chicken and dumplings and a pile of broccoli. "I'm going to need a bigger plate!" said Trevor.

Farrah wished for macaroni and cheese, a pealed orange, a banana, some cherries and strawberries, and a big helping of spaghetti with tomato sauce. All of this appeared on her plate, along with a big glass of milk. Trevor was drinking milk too, but his was chocolate.

"Wow, Banana, this is awesome!" said Trevor. "I bet everyone on your planet is really fat!" Trevor looked over to Banana Splash's plate and noticed that it was empty. "Aren't you going to eat anything?"

"I am eating," said Banana Splash. "I'm having the most amazing meal right now. It's being transported directly into my stomach. That's how we usually eat. Over the centuries, we've evolved to enjoy consuming exactly the right amount and kind of food. I'm glad you are enjoying your food too." With that, Banana let out a loud burp. "You're welcome," he said.

Professor Sparks laughed, along with everyone else. "See. I told you Banana was a lot of fun at parties!"

"When are we going to get some more Juicy Juicy lessons?" asked Trevor.

"Right after dinner," said Banana Splash. "But first, I have a riddle for you. Clear your mind. Don't assume anything. Are you ready?" Everyone nodded. "What jumps higher than a building?"

Farrah yelled out, "Superman?" Banana shook his head. Apparently fictional characters were not allowed in this riddle.

"Nothing!" said Trevor.

"Close," said Banana Splash, "Think deeply."

Professor Sparks smiled at Banana Splash. This was one of his favorite riddles.

Just then, Trevor answered the puzzle. "Everything! Everything and everyone jump higher than a building, because buildings can't jump at all!"

"You mean, everything that can jump," corrected Farrah, "jumps higher than a building. Good one!"

"Well done once again," said Banana Splash. "Good teamwork. Is everyone done with their meal? Who wants to learn some Juicy Juicy?"

Chapter 26: Hide and Seek

Everyone got up from the dinner table. "Where should we go for our Juicy Juicy lessons?" asked Trevor. "And when are you going to show us around the rest of your house?"

Banana Splash gestured in every direction. "This is my whole house. I can transform it into anything you like. Even though it stays small on the outside, we can make it as large as we like on the inside."

"Cool," said Trevor. "Can you make it as large as the Biltmore mansion in North Carolina, with two hundred and fifty rooms, spectacular spiral staircases, and huge wood-paneled libraries? We could get a great game of hide and seek going."

"Sure," said Banana Splash. With another flick of his wrist, Banana transformed his home once again, this time into what appeared to be a huge mansion. "But let's not play hide and seek. It would be too easy for me to find everyone."

"Too easy?" said Trevor. "On the contrary, Bananarama, there is no way you will be able to find us! Let's go Farrah!" Trevor and Farrah ran out of the door of the library room they had been in and entered a huge grand entrance room which had a ceiling one hundred feet high. Farrah ran up one spiral staircase, and Trevor the other.

Trevor ran from room to room to room. Some rooms were like libraries with books on the walls, and some had huge fireplaces. Others had their walls covered by priceless paintings, and others had magnificent beds in them for sleeping. Finally, he found a room with old suits of armor displayed, like knights used to wear long ago. "I know!" Trevor thought to himself, "I'll hide in one of the suits of armor! No one will ever think to look there!" Getting into the suit of armor was harder than Trevor had expected, but he was so far ahead of Banana Splash that he had plenty of time.

Once Trevor got into the suit, he was very quiet. He heard nothing except his own breathing. He was so tired from running through the mansion that it was hard not to breathe heavily. Then in the distance he heard footsteps. "Be super quiet," Trevor thought to himself. "Hold your breath if they come into this room."

Sure enough, Banana Splash walked into the room with Farrah and Professor Sparks. Banana had already found Farrah! Banana Splash then walked over to Trevor wearing the suit of armor and peeked into the helmet. He knocked on it two times with his fist as one would on a friend's front door. "Knock, knock," said Banana Splash. "Anyone home?"

Trevor lifted the faceguard on his helmet and stared at Banana Splash in disbelief. "How did you find us so quickly? If I hadn't seen it with my own eyes, I wouldn't have believed it! You walked straight to me!"

"Simple," said Banana Splash. "I used Juicy Juicy on you. Let me show you how you can do this too."

Chapter 30: Juicy Juicy

Trevor took off the suit of armor. "Here, hold this," said Banana Splash, who handed a small device to Trevor that looked like a calculator. "Now Farrah, you go run and hide anywhere in the house you like, and Trevor will come looking for you, all by himself. Just be careful not to hurt yourself – there are weapons on display in some of the rooms."

Farrah ran out of the room, down the hallway, and around the corner. They heard a door slam in the distance, and then another, even farther away. It was clear that Farrah was running far away to find her hiding place. "There's no way I'll ever find her," thought Trevor.

"The device in your hand is called a futurometer," said Banana Splash. "Go ahead. Ask it any probability question that you like."

"Okay," said Trevor, "What is the probability that I will find Farrah?" The futurometer read 100%. "Wow, neat," said Trevor. "But how does telling me that I will eventually find Farrah actually help me find Farrah?"

"Ask a more specific question," said Banana, "one whose answer is neither 100% nor 0%."

Trevor thought about this. "Okay, what is the probability that I will find Farrah in the next minute?" The futurometer read 19%. Trevor walked out the door and down the hallway down which Farrah had run. The futurometer read 23%. He went through some doors. 27%. He turned left, causing the futurometer to drop to 26%.

"You see, whenever you take a wrong turn, the futurometer tells you this by dropping the percentage chance of finding Farrah within the next minute. All you have to do is make choices which increase the probability of finding Farrah in the next minute," said Banana.

"Oh, I see," said Trevor. He took a right turn instead of his original left turn and the futurometer read 35%. Trevor started to run, leaving Professor Sparks and Banana Splash behind. 45%. At the end of the hallway were two staircases, one going up and one going down. Trevor chose the staircase going up. 43%. He turned around and took the stairs going down. 57%. Trevor ran down a hallway with 10 rooms on it. 65%. But when he passed by a large bedroom, the reading dropped to 64%. Trevor went back and entered the bedroom. 78%. The bedroom had a four-poster bed covered by a thin veil. "Cool bed," thought Trevor. "Would be kind of like sleeping in a tent." Trevor walked over to it. 77%. On the other side of the bedroom were various pieces of furniture, including a large wardrobe, which Trevor approached. 95%. "She must be in the wardrobe," thought Trevor to himself.

At the last second, Trevor hesitated, and thought to himself, "What if I purposely don't find Farrah? I'm just going to stand here for a minute and see what happens." Trevor stood perfectly still. 90%, 85%, 80%, 70%, read the futurometer. In an instant, Trevor changed his mind, grabbed the wardrobe's handle, and flung open the door. As he did this, the reading on the futurometer changed to 100%. "Surprise!" yelled Trevor. Sure enough, Farrah was in the wardrobe, stunned at how quickly Trevor had found her.

Just then, Banana Splash and Professor Sparks entered the room. "You did it!" said Professor Sparks. "Great job! Banana, can we all have one of these futurometers?"

"That old thing?" said Banana Splash. "That toy is for kids. I've got something much better for each of you."

Chapter 31: Special Pajamas

Banana Splash handed a pair of pajamas to Trevor, another pair to Farrah, and a bigger pair to Professor Sparks. "Night night time!" he joked. Fruit Smoothie also had 24 hour days, just like Earth.

"But I don't want to go to bed," said Farrah, jokingly.

"Well, these are very special pajamas," said Banana Splash. "These pajamas have Juicy Juicy built into them."

"Cool!" said Trevor, who put on his pajamas in front of everyone. Farrah went behind a screen to put on hers. The professor just held onto his, planning to put them on later. "Okay, now what do I do?" asked Trevor.

"Why, go to sleep, of course!" said Banana Splash. "Pick any bed in any room you like, make yourself comfortable, and then have a good night's sleep. See you in the morning!"

Trevor felt very disappointed. He had actually thought that these pajamas were special pajamas. Instead, he felt like a little kid whose mommy told him his pajamas were magic pajamas to get him to go to bed at night. Still, he *was* kind of tired.

"Good night, everyone!" said Trevor, who then went in search of the coolest bedroom he could find. He found a huge bed that was super comfy, got under the sheets, and fell asleep. He dreamed about what an amazing adventure he was on with his sister and his brother, even though they were all from different realities. He dreamed about his travels through space and time to new planets, and even a moon. He began to feel a oneness with the universe as he thought about its enormity and found a new appreciation for all forms of life, wherever they exist. Past, present, and future events swirled inside Trevor's mind, and the connection between them all seemed so clear.

When Trevor woke up the next morning, he felt refreshed and full of life. Today was the day he would learn Juicy Juicy. Someone knocked on the door. "Come in," said Trevor, as he sat up in his bed.

Banana Splash walked in, with Farrah and Professor Sparks, who were still wearing their pajamas. "By the way," said Banana, "I wasn't joking about these pajamas. They are indeed very special." With that, he took Professor Sparks's cane and hit Trevor's legs with a hard blow. The cane bounced off of Trevor's legs, flew from Banana's hand, and hit the ceiling before falling to the floor.

"I didn't feel a thing," said Trevor. "That was awesome!"

"While you were sleeping," said Banana, "these pajamas integrated themselves into your being. They protect you, even where they don't cover you. They also have a million times as much intuition as that old futurometer that we were playing around with last night. It's like having a bunch of futurometers, built into your head, answering every conceivable probability question for you. From now on, your intuition will be spot on. You'll understand the probabilities of what might happen, depending on the choices you make. Of course, it will still take discipline and courage to actually do what you think is right."

Trevor thought this all sounded terrific, but wasn't sure what to make of it.

"Be sure to use these pajamas responsibly," said Banana Splash, "because they have tremendous power. Now who wants breakfast?"

Chapter 32: Brush Your Teeth

"Banana, can we keep your house like the Biltmore Estate?" said Farrah. "I like this mansion a lot. I like my room, and it seems like a great place to practice playing hide and seek."

"Sure," said Banana Splash. "We just need to find the breakfast room. Who wants to find it for us?"

"Oh, I do!" said Trevor, who was putting his clothes on over his pajamas. "I'll use my pajamas to find it. I'm never taking these pajamas off, ever!"

Trevor had a strong feeling that the breakfast room was downstairs. He walked in the direction that seemed right to him, and then down a staircase. For a split second he almost took a wrong turn, but realized his mistake so fast that nobody noticed. He then walked over to a door at the end of a long hallway. "Here we are, the breakfast room!" announced Trevor, as he opened the door. A beautifully decorated table was centered in a majestic room with a spectacular view of the trees and hills of North Carolina. "Why does it look like North Carolina out the window?" asked Trevor.

"For your viewing pleasure, I had my house simulate the views out the windows of the Biltmore Estate," said Banana Splash, as he waved his hand. Once again, an empty plate and glass appeared in front of each seat at the breakfast table. "Enjoy your breakfast!" said Banana Splash. Everyone sat down at the table, imagined the perfect breakfast, and began to eat and drink.

"So, what do we have planned for today?" asked Trevor. "More Juicy Juicy lessons?"

"Indeed. I am taking you to meet my mentor, Master Lettuce Wraps. He is not only a Juicy Juicy Master, but also the leader of all of the Juicy Juicy Masters on my planet. It is a great honor for all of us that he has agreed to help with your instruction."

Trevor and Farrah were nervous about meeting such an important person, unlike Professor Sparks who was too old and accomplished to be nervous about much anymore. "We look forward to meeting him!" said Professor Sparks.

Farrah suddenly realized that she didn't have her toothbrush. "Banana, any chance that you have a toothbrush for each of us? I always brush my teeth after breakfast, especially when I want to look my best." Farrah had beautiful teeth.

With a flick of Banana's wrist, toothbrushes and combs appeared in front of each of the guests. "Sure," said Banana. "We brush our teeth too. Even though we don't usually chew food with our teeth, we live to be around five hundred years old, so brushing our teeth is very important too. In fact, our toothbrushes have Juicy Juicy built into them. Look."

Trevor looked at his toothbrush, which on the handle read, "You will have about 8 more cavities." Trevor felt embarrassed. He knew he should brush his teeth after every meal and floss every day, but he never flossed and often only brushed his teeth after breakfast, and then only because his parents told him too. He thought about sitting in the dentist's chair getting 8 cavities filled, with shots in his mouth and a dentist drilling on his teeth.

"I'm going to brush my teeth after every meal," thought Trevor, "and floss every night." When he looked again, his toothbrush read, "You will have about 0 more cavities."

"Much better!" thought Trevor.

Chapter 33: Wormholes

After breakfast, everyone took a bath, combed their hair, brushed their teeth, and got dressed. Under their clothes, Trevor, Farrah, and Professor Sparks wore their special pajamas which they noticed were air-cooled somehow so that they didn't get too hot or too cold, but were always the right temperature. Everyone met downstairs.

"On my planet, we use wormhole technology to get around," said Banana Splash. "This allows us to walk anywhere on our planet in about 30 minutes. Here, put on these special glasses so that you can read the signs."

Everyone followed Banana outside. Above his front door was what appeared to be his address: "Banana Splash, 601-523-115-234." There were seven houses in a circle centered around three arches that were 20 feet tall and 40 feet wide. Everyone followed Banana toward the nearest arch.

"You see, when we pass through this arch, we will not be in my neighborhood anymore, but instead will be in a completely different spot on my planet," said Banana. Sure enough, as the group approached the arch, they could see that there was something other than Banana's neighborhood on the other side. After they passed through it, the arch that they came out of was again one of three arches surrounded by seven completely different buildings in a new location with majestic mountains in the distance.

The group stayed close to Banana Splash, following him through the arch closest to the mountains. This led the group to a third location, also with three arches surrounded by seven new buildings, not too far from a beautiful lake. "Are we there yet?" asked Trevor.

"Not yet," said Banana Splash. We've got twenty more arches to pass through. Like everyone else, I'm using my Juicy Juicy to know which arches to pass through at each junction."

"Are you wearing Juicy Juicy pajamas under your clothes?" asked Trevor. "I don't see any."

"We used to," said Banana, "billions of years ago. But eventually our species evolved to the point that we are all born with Juicy Juicy, making special pajamas unnecessary for us. Some of us, like me, even have special abilities, like the ability to stop time."

Occasionally, at some of the junctions, the group saw other Fruit Smoothians, as well as a variety of other life forms, using the arch system to get to where they were going. "It gets pretty crowded in the mornings," said Banana Splash, "but the morning rush is over now."

"How many arch junctions are there on your planet?" asked Trevor.

"About a billion," said Banana Splash, "on my planet, as well as another three billion or so which interconnect us with eight other planets in our galaxy."

Trevor was shocked. "Are you telling me you can *walk* to other planets? And in only a few minutes, from your *home*? That's so cool!"

"Absolutely," said Banana Splash. "Walking is a great form of exercise. I enjoy walking places whenever I can. It's good for you, and it's very refreshing. In fact, that's how I got to the Café Mobius the night we met."

Chapter 34: Master Lettuce Wraps

After Trevor, Farrah, Professor Sparks, and Banana Splash walked through the last arch, they found themselves approaching a very tall building that looked like it might be a hundred stories tall. "Here we are, District Headquarters!" said Banana Splash.

They entered through the front door into a lobby made out of marble with a very high ceiling. Everyone followed Banana Splash across the lobby into an elevator. Banana then put a special key into the elevator and pushed a complicated sequence of buttons. "Master Lettuce Wraps is on B343, which is 343 stories underground," said Banana. "This is a top secret location, so don't tell anyone about these underground floors, or that you met Master Wraps. Even though we've been a peaceful planet for billions of years, we still have criminals, some very dangerous, as well as spies from other planets from time to time. We even had a little skirmish with another planet ten million years ago."

Everyone followed Banana Splash out of the elevator and across a large room filled with dozens of Fruit Smoothians. Everyone in the room stopped what they were doing and stared at Trevor. "Why is everyone staring at me?" asked Trevor.

"Well, there is something I should tell you," said Banana Splash. "Our meeting at the Café Mobius was not an accident, nor was my friendship with Professor Sparks before that."

"I am indeed a friend to all of you, just like you think I am, but I am also working for my planet. You see, somehow, someway, Trevor ..." Banana paused, like he wasn't sure how to say what he wanted to say, "you are going to save my planet, and everyone on it."

Trevor was shocked. Who was Banana Splash - some kind of secret agent? Trevor used his Juicy Juicy and realized that Banana was telling the truth. He pulled out the futurometer from his pocket and asked it directly, "What is the probability that I will save the planet Fruit Smoothie?" The futurometer read 50%. "The futurometer says that there is only a 50% chance that I will save your planet," said Trevor. The group entered an important looking office.

"That is why you are here," said a large Fruit Smoothian wearing important looking clothes. "Hi, I am Master Lettuce Wraps." Master Wraps shook Trevor's hand, then Farrah's, and then Professor Sparks's and Banana Splash's. "Great to see you, Agent Splash. Everyone, please, sit down. Make yourselves comfortable."

Master Wraps sat in a chair opposite Trevor. "Trevor, as the head of security for my planet, as well as an ordinary citizen with family and friends who are good people ..." Master Lettuce Wraps started to get emotional, but then regained his composure. "I am begging you ..." He paused, and then got down on one knee. He reached out with both of his hands to hold Trevor's right hand. "Will you save our planet?"

Trevor was stunned. "Sure, I guess," said Trevor, who was still having a hard time understanding the situation. "What do I need to do?"

"That's the thing," said Master Wraps, who looked away, and then back at Trevor. "We don't know."

Chapter 35: Walkie Talkies

"We figure the best idea is to be ready for anything," said Master Wraps. "First of all, Trevor, I am going to give you a walkie talkie. If you ever need anything, push the button, day or night, and I will get a team of highly trained secret agents on it right away."

Trevor and Farrah loved walkie talkies, and already owned a pair at home that they used to talk with the kids next door. "Cool, thanks," said Trevor.

"Second, we'd like to enroll you in our secret agent training program," said Master Wraps. "We have the best secret agent training program in the galaxy, which is one of the reasons we've enjoyed peace and prosperity on our planet for billions of years."

"I'm in," said Trevor.

"Me too," said Farrah.

Master Wraps chuckled. "Farrah, you're a girl, and only nine years old. This training will be way too hard for you." Trevor grimaced. Obviously this guy didn't know Farrah very well.

"What?" exclaimed Farrah. "I can do anything Trevor can do. I want to be a secret agent too!"

Trevor supported his sister. "Farrah gets to do everything I do, or I'm going home," said Trevor. "We're a team."

"Okay, okay," said Master Wraps, who seemed willing to agree to anything. "Whatever you want."

"And I get a walkie talkie," said Farrah.

"Absolutely, you get a walkie talkie," said Master Wraps.

"And a flying unicorn who can talk, read minds, and grant wishes," said Farrah.

Trevor grimaced again. He had never heard of such a ridiculous request. It reminded him of the ridiculous dream he had dreamt about Farrah and a unicorn.

"Sure, we can do that," said Master Wraps, "as soon as you complete your training." Trevor couldn't believe his ears. Even Farrah was surprised, but didn't reveal it.

"One last thing," said Master Wraps. "It's best if each of you has a code name. If we encounter bad guys, we don't want them finding out where you live, if you know what I mean."

"Makes sense," said Professor Sparks. "We've got a lot of family back home to protect."

"I'll be Trevor the Time Traveler," said Trevor.

"And I'll be Farrah the Fairy Princess," said Farrah. "But you can just call me Princess Farrah, for short, if you like." Trevor smiled. His sister was on a roll.

"All right, your code names will be Time Traveler and Fairy Princess," said Master Wraps. "Now let's get you off to training camp."

Chapter 36: Training Camp

"I'm going to sit this training camp out," said Professor Sparks, "but I'll watch you every step of the way. I want to help, but fighting and weapons are not for an old man like me." Trevor and Farrah understood.

Trevor's watch read 10 a.m. as they entered the training camp on floor B344 of the building, 344 stories underground. They had two instructors, Sweet Chili, who led the classroom instruction, and Hot Mustard, who was in charge of martial arts and weapons. Day One was all classroom instruction, much to Trevor's and Farrah's disappointment. "When are we going to get to try out some weapons?" thought Trevor.

"Tomorrow," replied Sweet Chili inside Trevor's mind. Sweet Chili was a friendly female Fruit Smoothian who could read minds and talk inside people's heads. "Today we're making you smart. Tomorrow we'll make you strong." Trevor noticed that Sweet Chili and Farrah were becoming good friends.

The rest of the day was all about weapons safety and codes that secret agents needed to know. Trevor and Farrah took careful notes. The Juicy Juicy in their pajamas told them that learning a little now would pay off big later.

When all of the classes were over for the day, Master Wraps came by to see how things were going. "Feeling smarter yet?" he joked.

"I've never studied harder in my life," said Trevor. Farrah nodded in agreement.

"Great. We have one other suggestion for you, which we think you will appreciate. We suggest that you alternate days between our training camp on Fruit Smoothie and your own school work back home on Earth. You're doing great, but we want you happy and here for the long haul. Sound good?"

"Great idea!" said Farrah. Trevor agreed.

"Okay, then, see you tomorrow," said Master Wraps.

"But we'll be in school tomorrow, back on Earth," said Farrah.

"No, you'll be in school tomorrow, ten thousand years ago," replied Master Wraps. "Remember, we're ten thousand years in the future, from your home's perspective. Just set your time machine to come back one second after it leaves, and it will be like you never left."

"Right!" said Trevor. "Time machines are so awesome!"

Trevor and Farrah met back up with Professor Sparks and Banana Splash and told them about all the cool things they were learning. As they left the building at 4 p.m., Trevor pushed the button on his remote control and his time machine appeared before them. "See you in one second," said Trevor, as he and Farrah got in. His minivan time machine disappeared as it dropped off and then picked up Trevor and Farrah one day later from their home realities, and then reappeared on Fruit Smoothie, one second after it had left. Trevor and Farrah got out. His minivan time machine disappeared when Trevor pushed the button on his remote again.

"Sure was nice to sleep in my own bed," said Farrah, "and to see my family. The other Trevor told me to say hi to everyone, by the way."

Trevor nodded. "And I tried extra hard in school today," said Trevor, "and asked for extra work. I want to get smart as fast as I can."

The four friends started walking back to Banana's home. "But it is also great to be back," said Trevor. "I can't wait for Weapons Day tomorrow."

61

Chapter 40: Code Red

After a great evening of talking, relaxing, and playing at Banana's house and a very good night's sleep, Trevor and Farrah showed up bright and early for Day Two of their secret agent training camp at District Headquarters. Their instructor for the day was Hot Mustard, a huge Fruit Smoothian who was an expert at combat. Everything about him was very scary. There were seven other students in the training camp besides Trevor and Farrah, all full grown Fruit Smoothians, and all very strong looking.

"You will do exactly as I say," yelled Hot Mustard, "or people here might get killed! Do you understand me?"

All of the students yelled, "Yes sir, Hot Mustard!" as loud as they could. This was Trevor's and Farrah's favorite part.

The day began with hand to hand combat. Everyone put on wrestling helmets for safety, and students paired up to wrestle against each other. Trevor and Farrah got each other. Some unlucky student got Hot Mustard.

"The key to hand to hand combat," yelled Hot Mustard, "is knowing what your opponent is going to do before they do!" With that, he turned to his student opponent and told him to attack. The student lunged forward, trying to grab Hot Mustard. Instead, Hot Mustard tripped his opponent, pinned him on the ground, and stuck his opponent's foot into his own ear. It would have been very funny had every student not been afraid that Hot Mustard might do that to them, too.

Trevor didn't like bullies, so it bothered Trevor the way Hot Mustard was so hard on the student he fought. "I bet I can beat you!" yelled Trevor. Farrah looked at him like he was crazy.

"Ah, our honored guest wants to fight me! Very brave, but not very bright, I'm afraid. Sit down, young man," said Hot Mustard, "Spare yourself the embarrassment."

"I will not sit down!" said Trevor. "I want to fight you. How else am I going to learn if you don't let me practice?" Hot Mustard looked confused. He wasn't used to being challenged.

"Okay, have it your way." He motioned for Trevor to come up to the front and join him on the mat. They stood ten feet apart, staring at each other. Trevor instinctively hid his thoughts from Hot Mustard, who was trying to read his mind, trying to see what Trevor was up to. "Ready?" said Hot Mustard. "Go!"

Hot Mustard ran straight toward Trevor, who pulled out his walkie talkie and yelled, "Code Red, Code Red!" Immediately three highly trained secret agents appeared out of thin air, grabbed Hot Mustard, and pinned him to the ground.

"Hey, that's not fair," yelled Hot Mustard, who was pinned under three secret agents.

"Just for that, stick his foot in his ear," said Trevor to the secret agents, who followed his every command. Everyone laughed. Farrah was laughing so hard she was rolling on the ground.

"All right, I give up, you win!" said Hot Mustard as he laughed, clearly amused at having been beaten. Trevor motioned to the secret agents to let Hot Mustard up, who came over and shook Trevor's hand.

"Well done, son," said Hot Mustard. "Someday, when you save our planet, nobody is going to care how you did it. You keep learning those codes!"

"Yes, sir," said Trevor. "And thank you for the practice!"

Chapter 41: Weapons Day

The next two hours focused on martial arts techniques. Trevor and Farrah practiced with each other, learning how to keep their balance and how to use the other person's size and momentum against them. They were both getting very good at wrestling.

"With these techniques, and much more practice," said Hot Mustard, "you'll be able to take down someone twice your size." Trevor and Farrah liked the sound of that. "And with the practice you'll receive from us over the coming days, you'll even be able to put their foot in their ear." Everyone laughed. Trevor and Farrah were beginning to like Hot Mustard a lot.

After lunch, the class met at the underground firing range. Everyone in the class wore protective goggles and was on one side of a barrier about four feet high. The other side of the room was a no man's land of dirt and rock with huge craters that seemed to have been created by exploding bombs. Paper targets were set up in the distance, and mannequins dressed up like bad guys were placed throughout.

Hot Mustard held up a huge gun. "The Dematerializer," he said in a loud voice, "does just what its name says." He fired it at a mannequin, which ceased to exist. "Very powerful, very deadly, but not very good for asking bad guys questions later."

Hot Mustard held up an even bigger gun. "The Liquefier." He fired it at another one of the mannequins, which turned to goo, leaving a puddle on the ground. "Kind of like the first gun, but you can test that goo later to identify the bad guy. Just don't use it on your mom's carpet – there's no way to get that stain out."

"The Atom Smasher." Hot Mustard held up a tiny little gun, and then fired it at another mannequin, which exploded violently into a billion little pieces. "Messy, but effective."

"The Vaporizer." Hot Mustard held up another small gun, fired it, and turned another mannequin into a whiff of smoke. "Don't breathe in the smoke. Depending on the target, it can be bad for your lungs."

"Cool as these guns are, none of them are standard issue," said Hot Mustard. "Our secret agents only use non-lethal devices, like the ones I am about to show you, for two reasons. First, we haven't killed an innocent bystander or anyone else in two million years. Second, after we arrest bad guys, we like to read their minds to see what other information we can gather."

"The Chunkifier," said Hot Mustard, who held up a gun that kind of looked like a piece of pepperoni pizza to Trevor, but with a handle and trigger on it, "multiplies the weight of what it hits by seven." He fired the gun at a mannequin. The mannequin expanded in every direction, and then collapsed under its own weight. "We can dechunkify bad guys later, but it takes a while," said Hot Mustard. "Don't use this weapon lightly. It's very uncomfortable for whomever you hit."

"Now, for the grand finale, the moment you've all been waiting for," said Hot Mustard. "The Ho-mol-o-gi-zer," he said slowly, sounding like huh-mall-uh-jie-zer. "The homologizer is our standard issue, solve-every-problem-right-now device." He held up something so small no one could even see it. He fired it at a mannequin. A silvery rubber band came out of the device, expanded, went around the mannequin, and then closed up, leaving nothing behind. "Bingo!" said Hot Mustard. "Problem solved."

Trevor raised his hand. "I thought you said this gun was non-lethal?"

"It is," said Hot Mustard. "In fact, technically it's not even a gun. That was a wormhole that went around the target, the same technology used in our arches. Mr. Mannequin is in a holding cell on B686. Secret agents are trying to read his mind right now. Come on, let's go take a look."

65

Chapter 42: Homologizers

As the class took the elevator down to B686, Hot Mustard continued the lesson. "Homologizers, used properly, are perfectly safe. They are also so small that we can implant them into any ordinary item that you like."

"Like a watch?" asked Trevor.

"Or a purse?" asked Farrah.

"Sure, either of those is fine," said Hot Mustard. "For a secret agent, surprise is important, so the more ordinary the item, the better."

The class followed Hot Mustard into level B686, which was a huge room with holding cells all around the perimeter. "These holding cells are only temporary," said Hot Mustard. "We don't keep prisoners here for very long – just long enough to read their minds and, if necessary, to erase any dangerous memories. Then we give them as much counseling and training as they need to be nice next time and send them on their way." Hot Mustard paused. "As rough and tough as we are, our first choice is to teach people how to behave in a civilized society, and to reward them for trying to do the right thing. It doesn't always work, but we try."

The class followed Hot Mustard to the holding cell with Mr. Mannequin, who was perfectly fine. Some secret agents were gathered around. "Having some fun with the mannequins today?" asked one of them.

"Yeah, today is Weapons Day," said Hot Mustard. "We're learning how to use homologizers." Hot Mustard turned to the class. "Now I want everyone to pick an ordinary item that you already have on you, and I'll implant your homologizer on that item for you."

Trevor held out his watch. Hot Mustard used a pair of tweezers to hold the homologizer which automatically fused with Trevor's watch. Farrah then showed Hot Mustard where she wanted her homologizer placed on her purse, which she always carried with her. Other students used pens, glasses, and even shoes.

"I need a volunteer," said Hot Mustard. Farrah raised her hand. Hot Mustard pointed at her and motioned for her to come to the front of the group. "Okay, Farrah, shoot me. That's right, shoot ..."

Before Hot Mustard could finish his sentence, Farrah shot her homologizer at Hot Mustard. She felt her mind controlling the silvery rubber band which came out of her homologizer and directed it to enclose Hot Mustard, which it did, causing him to disappear in an instant.

"And that's how easy it is," yelled Hot Mustard, who was now in a holding cell across the room. The secret agents went over to the cell and let him out. "Any questions?"

Farrah spoke up. "It felt like I was using my mind to direct the wormhole. Was I really doing that?"

"Yes you were," said Hot Mustard. "Like your Juicy Juicy pajamas, your homologizer integrates with your mind. You control the wormhole that comes out with your mind, and can even choose to transport your target wherever you like, though these holding cells are usually the best place."

"Any other questions?" asked Hot Mustard. No one said anything. "Okay, then, spread out. We're going to play a game. Last person standing wins."

Chapter 43: Free for All

"The rules for this game are simple," said Hot Mustard. "You may only fire wormholes at each other. If you find yourself in one of the holding cells along the sides of the room, you are out. The last person standing in the middle of the room wins."

Trevor and Farrah were shocked, but instinctively turned their backs to each other. "I'll protect your back if you protect mine," said Trevor.

Farrah nodded in agreement, and whispered, "When I shot my homologizer at Hot Mustard, I realized that I could make the wormhole as large as I liked," said Farrah. "See if you can enclose everyone on your side of the room, all at once, with a wormhole that goes all the way to the top of the room. I'll do the same." Trevor thought this was a great idea.

"On your mark, get set, go!" yelled Hot Mustard. Immediately Hot Mustard and every student in the room began firing at each other. Wormholes headed in every direction, including one that was heading straight for Trevor.

Trevor fired the homologizer in his watch at the wormhole coming toward him. A small, silvery wormhole came out which Trevor controlled with his mind. Trevor's wormhole got very large, as large as the room itself, and enclosed everyone and everything on his side of the room. Then it shrank to nothing, and everyone was gone.

Trevor turned around to see that Farrah had successfully employed the same strategy, and that everyone else was in a holding cell, including the secret agents who weren't even playing. "Hey, you weren't supposed to shoot us!" they yelled.

"Sorry," said Trevor and Farrah.

Trevor held up his hand, and Farrah gave him a high five. "Yea, we did it!" yelled Trevor. "Do we get a prize?"

"The winner of the contest gets a very special prize - a wand that can make anything invisible," replied Hot Mustard from his cell. "But the contest is not over. There are still two people left standing in the middle of the room."

Trevor and Farrah looked at each other. Both wanted the prize very much. "It was your idea that won us the contest," Trevor said to Farrah. "Go ahead and shoot me."

Farrah pointed her purse at Trevor, but just couldn't do it. "I wouldn't even be here if you hadn't stood up for me in Master Wraps's office. You should get the prize. Go ahead and shoot me."

Hot Mustard couldn't believe his ears. "What are you guys talking about? Someone shoot somebody already!" Trevor and Farrah ignored him.

"I have an idea!" said Trevor. "Let's flip for it. Heads I win, tails you win." Farrah nodded in agreement.

Trevor pulled out a quarter from his pocket and flipped it. Farrah gasped when she saw it was tails. "Yea, I win!" she exclaimed. Trevor was disappointed, but happy to see his sister so excited. "Sorry about this," said Farrah, who then shot Trevor with a wormhole from her homologizer.

"That's okay," yelled Trevor from his holding cell across the room. "Just don't ever turn me invisible without asking me first!"

"Farrah the Fairy Princess wins!" announced Hot Mustard. "Now come over here and let all of us out!"

69

Chapter 44: Playing Outside

Trevor and Farrah met up with Professor Sparks and Banana Splash to tell them everything that had happened. The four of them left District Headquarters together.

"What a great day!" exclaimed Farrah, who was showing her invisibility wand to everyone. She turned herself invisible with her wand, snuck up behind Trevor, and spanked him on the rear as hard as she could.

"Hey!" said Trevor. Farrah reappeared, laughing and smiling. Trevor laughed too.

As they did every day at 4 p.m., Trevor and Farrah got into Trevor's time machine. "Bye, Professor, bye Banana! See you in one second," said Trevor.

Trevor and Farrah put on their seatbelts. "Jeeves, take us to Farrah's home reality, ten thousand years ago, one second after she left," said Trevor. The minivan began its journey across the multiverse, disappearing in an instant from the point of view of Professor Sparks and Banana Splash, but smoothly accelerating into outer space from the point of view of Trevor and Farrah.

"Trevor, thank you so much!" said Farrah, who leaned over to give him a big hug. "I'm having such a great time!" Trevor enjoyed seeing his sister so happy. "If you ever need anyone or anything turned invisible, just let me know!"

The time machine arrived at Farrah's reality, parked around the corner from their house. "Bye!" said Farrah, as she exited the car.

"Bye!" said Trevor. Farrah closed the door and made her way home. "Jeeves, take me to my home reality, one second after I left," said Trevor. The time machine seemed to stay motionless, but the light outside flickered randomly as the time machine passed through different realities, each with its own weather. The time machine stopped. "Here we are," said Jeeves.

Trevor thought how glad he was to be home as he got out of the minivan, which was still parked around the corner from his house. He pushed the button on his remote, causing it to disappear. His watch, which kept track of the days of the week as well as the time, said "Thursday, 4 p.m." Trevor reminded himself, however, that it was actually only Tuesday at 4 p.m. back on Earth because he and his watch had spent two awesome days on Fruit Smoothie.

As Trevor approached his house, he saw that the kids next door were playing outside with Farrah and Roo. Roo was playing with Aaron, and Farrah was playing jump rope with Allie. Trevor reminded himself that this Farrah hadn't been to Fruit Smoothie and didn't even know about his time machine, which he was supposed to keep a secret.

"Where have you been?" asked Roo.

"Oh, I just went for a short walk," said Trevor.

"Okay," said Roo, who ran off with Aaron. They were collecting frogs in a big bucket.

"Hey Alex, want to see something cool?" said Trevor. Alex, who had been playing basketball in Trevor's driveway, dropped the ball and ran over.

"Yeah, man, what's up?"

Chapter 45: Best Friends

Trevor took the futurometer, which kind of looked like a calculator, out of his pocket.

"What's that?" asked Alex.

"Can you keep a secret?" asked Trevor.

"Sure, no problem," said Alex.

"It's a futurometer," said Trevor. "You can ask it any probability question that you want, and it will tell you the answer. And my watch is a homologizer that shoots wormholes."

Alex laughed. "Cool. My watch is a homologizer too." Alex pretended to shoot Trevor with his watch. "Patew, patew!" said Alex.

Trevor thought how lucky he was to live next door to his best friend. He then thought how hard it was to keep secrets, and how he might be putting Alex in danger if Trevor told him his secrets.

"Patew, patew!" said Trevor, who pretended to shoot at Alex with his watch. The two of them ran off together, pretending to shoot at each other.

"Hey, Trevor," said Alex. "Are you wearing your pajamas under your clothes?" Trevor's pajamas had a collar on them that stuck out the neck hole of his shirt.

"Yep," said Trevor. "They're awesome. They have Juicy Juicy built into them. I'm never going to take them off again!"

Alex fell down laughing. "Juicy, juicy!" he said back to Trevor, who was laughing too. "I'm going to go put on my pajamas, too!" Alex ran inside.

Trevor looked over and saw Farrah, still jumping rope and singing songs with Allie. They were best friends too, as were Roo and Aaron. Roo and Aaron had seven frogs in their bucket, one of their best days ever.

Trevor enjoyed the moment. "Ahhh," he thought to himself, "Home."

Alex came running out of his house, with his pajamas under his clothes too. "I'm never going to take off my pajamas either!" Trevor and Alex laughed together until it hurt. All six kids played outside for the rest of the day.

"Kids, dinner time!" yelled Alex's mom.

"See you, Trevor," said Alex.

"Bye, Alex," said Trevor.

Alex, Allie, and Aaron ran inside their house. Farrah and Roo came over to Trevor. Trevor missed both of them so much that he gave both of them big hugs.

"Quit it," said Roo, laughing.

Farrah just smiled.

"I love you guys," said Trevor.

Chapter 46: Bullies

The next day at school was a Wednesday. Trevor tried extra hard in his fifth grade class, just as he had the previous school day. He even asked for extra work. "I'm trying to get as smart as I can," said Trevor to his teacher, Mrs. Smart.

"That's wonderful," said Mrs. Smart. "The harder you try, the smarter you'll get!" She liked enthusiastic students.

Trevor liked all of his teachers. He had Mrs. Smart for reading, language arts, and social studies, Mrs. Newton for math and science, and Mrs. Lily for music and art. Trevor also got thirty minutes for playing outside during recess every day and thirty minutes for lunch in the cafeteria.

The only thing Trevor didn't like about his school was a sixth grader named Tommy. Some of Trevor's friends had been hurt by Tommy, who liked to sit on smaller kids during recess. All of Trevor's friends were scared of him. Trevor had been scared of him too, but he wasn't scared any more.

"I'm coming to get you!" yelled Tommy, who grabbed one of the smaller second graders. Tommy sat on him and started laughing.

"Hey, get off of him," yelled Trevor. The other fifth graders looked at Trevor like he was crazy. "Get off of him right now!"

Tommy looked confused. He wasn't used to being challenged. "What did you say?"

"I said get off of him right now!" said Trevor.

Tommy got up and walked over to Trevor. "You're not very smart, are you?" said Tommy, who saw Trevor's pajamas sticking out of his shirt. "Why do you wear your pajamas to school, pajama boy? Does your mommy make you?"

Tommy pushed Trevor on the chest, trying to knock him down. But Trevor just stood there, with Tommy pushing on Trevor like someone pushing against a telephone pole. Tommy pushed harder, until he was red in the face. "Why won't you fall down!" yelled Tommy.

Trevor thought about his training in martial arts class. He moved to the side and pulled on Tommy's arm, causing him to fall to the ground. Then he walked over to Tommy and sat on him. Trevor's pajamas held down Tommy, who was stuck like a bug under a rock.

"Whoa," said the other fifth graders. "Trevor beat up Tommy!" They all ran off to tell their friends.

"You know, you should always be nice," said Trevor. "And you shouldn't sit on smaller kids. It scares them a lot."

"Okay, okay, just let me up," gasped Tommy, who was flailing his arms and legs. "Just let me up!"

Trevor let Tommy up. "Don't sit on any more kids," said Trevor, as he walked off.

Tommy, embarrassed by having been beaten by a fifth grader, began to fill with rage. "Arrrrrrrrrgh!" yelled Tommy, as he ran toward Trevor as fast as he could. He was going to tackle Trevor.

Trevor turned and fired the homologizer in his watch. A silvery wormhole came out and went around Tommy, which then shrank down to nothing. Tommy was gone.

Chapter 50: A Good Attitude

"Whoops!" thought Trevor. "How am I going to explain this to my teachers?" Trevor realized that a missing student was a very serious thing, and that he probably shouldn't have sent Tommy to a holding cell deep underground on a distant planet to be thoroughly questioned by the security forces of the most technologically advanced civilization in the galaxy, ten thousand years in the future. "I might get into trouble for this," thought Trevor.

Mrs. Smart came running up. "Trevor, are you okay? I heard there was a fight between you and Tommy." She looked around. "Where is Tommy?"

Trevor was really embarrassed. He didn't like the idea of lying to his teacher, but she probably wouldn't even believe the truth. "Uh," said Trevor, "he's ..."

"I'm right here," said Tommy, who walked from around the corner of the building. "I attacked a second grader and sat on him, and then I tried to tackle Trevor. I want to apologize to everyone involved for my bad behavior." Tommy stood up straight and took a deep breath. He seemed much more confident and relaxed than his usual self.

Tommy continued. "What I did was wrong. I won't ever do it again." Tommy went over to the second grader he had sat on and extended his hand. The second grader shook it. He then went over to Trevor, who shook his hand too.

Everyone was stunned. Tommy was a changed boy who now seemed friendly, responsible, and mature. Trevor was impressed. The Fruit Smoothians really knew how to bring out the best in a boy.

"Well, as long as no one was hurt," said Mrs. Smart. "Everyone go back to class. Tommy, I'm impressed with your attitude, but I still have to punish you. After school, I want you to clean all of the chalkboard erasers in the entire school. I'll call your mom to tell her you'll be staying late."

"Yes, ma'am, Mrs. Smart, I will be happy to. Would you like me to erase all of the chalkboards as well? If you want, I would be happy to sweep the floors, too."

Mrs. Smart couldn't believe her ears. Tommy was beginning to sound like the student with the most positive attitude in the entire school. "Why, yes, thank you, Tommy, that would be very nice!"

As the students went back inside the school building, Tommy walked over to Trevor and whispered, "Thank you, Trevor, you've changed my whole life, and for the better."

Trevor used his Juicy Juicy and knew it was true. "You're welcome, Tommy. I hope we can be friends."

"Friends?" said Tommy, who suddenly got emotional. Tommy gave Trevor a hug. "Thank you, Trevor, from the bottom of my heart. You truly are a great person." He looked away, and then back at Trevor. "If you ever need anything - anything at all - just let me know."

Chapter 51: Do the Right Thing

After Trevor got home from school, he was surprised to see his dad, who had come home early from work, standing in the driveway. "Trevor, I heard you were in a fight," said his dad, "Are you okay?"

"Yes, I'm fine," said Trevor, "but it was pretty scary for a moment." Trevor thought how to phrase his words just right. "For a second, I thought I might have hurt the other kid very badly."

"Trevor," said his dad, "let's go for a walk together, around the neighborhood."

"Sure, dad," said Trevor. They walked down the driveway and then along the sidewalk.

"Trevor," said his dad, "Do you think you did the right thing?"

Trevor thought for a second. "Mostly," said Trevor. "I helped the second grader, but I could have hurt the sixth grader. I feel sorry about that."

"I'm glad you are thinking about this, Trevor," said his dad. "We are all defined by the choices we make in life. Good people are people who choose to make the world a better place, in every possible way, no matter how small, with every decision they make."

"Like choosing to help that second grader?" said Trevor.

"Absolutely," said Trevor's dad. "Or here's another example: after this walk, you can either do an extra good job on your homework, or you can skip your homework and just watch television. Which choice do you think will make the world a better place, in the long run?"

Trevor couldn't help but joke around. "TV," said Trevor, trying to get a reaction from his dad, who smiled. "Just joking. Doing a great job on my homework, of course." Trevor's dad smiled again.

"Yes, and do you know why?" said his dad.

"Because I will grow up smarter?" said Trevor.

"True," said Trevor's dad, "but why is that important?"

Trevor thought for a bit, and then shrugged his shoulders.

"Because the smarter you are, the more good things you'll know how to do," said his dad. "Sometimes, if you do lots of good things for people, they may even pay you money in return, or do something nice for you," continued his dad, "which is also good. After all, you are part of the world too, just not all of it."

"I see," said Trevor.

"I encourage you to think this way about every choice you make in your life," said Trevor's dad, "even with the smallest of decisions. If you can make someone else feel good by saying something nice to them, then do it. If you can help someone else learn an important idea, then do that too. If you are working on something, then do an extra good job. These small decisions seem trivial when considered one at a time, but over the course of your life, they add up. If you always try to do the right thing, every single time you have a choice to make, you will be a very happy and successful person."

"I see," said Trevor.

"One last thing," said Trevor's dad. "Don't think it is okay to only try to do the right thing some of the time. We all make mistakes, but once you start thinking like that you'll find reasons to do the wrong thing more and more often. Someday you may look up and realize that you are not the person you want to be. As a child, everyone starts out sweet and wonderful, but not everyone stays that way."

Trevor took his dad's advice very seriously. "I'm always going to try to do the right thing," said Trevor. "Always."

Chapter 52: Intelligence Briefing

"I'm going to do a great job on my homework," thought Trevor to himself, "as soon as I get back from trying to save the Fruit Smoothians." It was 4 p.m. again – time to get back to his secret agent training camp. Trevor got into his time machine and picked up Farrah on his way back to Fruit Smoothie, ten thousand years in the future. They arrived one second after they had left, just outside District Headquarters, where Professor Sparks and Banana Splash were still standing.

"How were your days back home?" asked Professor Sparks.

"I had some fun with my invisibility wand," said Farrah, "I was playing hide and seek with some friends, and nobody could find me. They never could figure out what happened!"

"I got into a fight with a kid at school," said Trevor, who wasn't too proud of what had happened. "Long story short - I'm guessing he's in a holding cell on B686 right now."

Banana Splash laughed. "You did what!" said Banana. "You're crazier than I am!"

Trevor told everyone all about it on the way back to Banana's house. Trevor and Farrah went to bed early so that they would be feeling their best for Day Three of training camp which began the next day.

Day Three started with an intelligence briefing. Banana Splash was leading the meeting, which included Trevor's and Farrah's class and fifty other secret agents, all looking very serious. Even Master Lettuce Wraps was there.

"Three days ago, Trevor, Farrah, Professor Sparks, and I stopped a terrorist attack at the Café Mobius on the planet Allegro. We've just received very alarming information about the bomb that we stopped from detonating. What we thought at first was an ordinary bomb is, instead, a new kind of bomb, beyond our understanding. In fact, the technology in the bomb is so advanced that we do not think it originated in our galaxy." Everyone gasped.

"What does the bomb do?" asked Professor Sparks.

"It is hard for us to say exactly," said Banana Splash, "without actually seeing the device explode. However, our best guess is that whoever detonates this bomb would be able to control everyone and everything within the blast radius of the bomb. This bomb doesn't kill people, it controls people. We're calling it a free will bomb."

Professor Sparks spoke up. "That's ridiculous. You always have free will, no matter what. It's a basic law of physics!"

"That's what we thought too," said Banana Splash, "but this technology is right at the edge of what we understand about the universe. We think this bomb can collapse huge sections of the multiverse, merging infinitely many universes into a single one, thereby destroying free will. Essentially, whoever sets off this bomb can choose the future they want, for everyone."

Everyone in the room was very alarmed. No one had ever heard of technology like this before, and no one seemed to know what to do. They all looked at Trevor.

Trevor saw all of the people who were counting on him. For a moment he wondered what he was doing on a far-away planet helping an alien race. Then he remembered his dad's advice about making the world a better place. He figured his dad would want him to make the universe a better place too. "Well," said Trevor, "it's simple. Let's find out who's responsible for this, and then stop them before it's too late!"

Chapter 53: Brainstorming

"I implanted tracking devices in the aliens who delivered the bomb to the Café Mobius," said Banana Splash. "We tracked them to their home planet, a planet called Org, in the Andromeda galaxy. These aliens seem to be very poor and not very bright. I don't even think they knew they were carrying a bomb, and probably would have been victims of the bomb too, had it gone off."

"I see," said Master Wraps, "So, have you figured out who gave them the bomb?"

"We're working on that," said Banana Splash. "We're getting a team together to go back in time to figure this out right now."

"Oh, I want to go," said Farrah.

"I'm in too," said Trevor.

"Me too," said Professor Sparks. "I feel responsible for you kids."

"Wait a second," said Master Wraps, "you kids haven't completed your training yet!" He thought a bit. "I don't like it. We shouldn't be risking important assets like this. We need a better plan." Everyone respected Master Wraps's wisdom and listened to what he had to say.

"Let's figure this out together," said Master Wraps, "like someone would solve a riddle." He paused. "We have advanced technology, not seen in this galaxy, and we have three aliens from the Andromeda galaxy. What can we conclude from this? What makes sense?"

"What do we know about the Andromeda galaxy?" asked Trevor.

"For the most part," said Master Wraps, "it is not very advanced, so we usually don't have any reason to go there. There are 5,012 planets with intelligent life, but only three of them have time traveling technology. One of those three, the planet Murkos, rules the Andromeda galaxy with an iron fist. They take what they want, including whole planets, and have no regard for other life forms."

"Is the Earth in danger?" asked Farrah. "Do we need to worry about the Murkians taking over the Earth and other planets in the Milky Way galaxy?"

"They'd like to do it, I'm sure of it," said Master Wraps. "But the 3,278 planets with intelligent life in the Milky Way galaxy are under our protection. The Murkians know to keep out. They would never challenge us again because they know our Juicy Juicy is so much stronger than their technology."

"Wait, that's it!" said Professor Sparks. "Juicy Juicy only tells you what is likely to happen as a result of choices you might make. But it takes free will to be able to make choices. If this free will bomb really works," said the professor, "your Juicy Juicy would be useless."

Master Wraps perked up. "I see. Somehow, someway, the Murkians must have found a way to neutralize our Juicy Juicy. If they could detonate free will bombs everywhere," said Master Wraps, "we'd be defenseless."

"And once they took over Fruit Smoothie …" said Professor Sparks.

Farrah interrupted, "There would be nothing stopping them from taking over the Earth, and every other planet in the Milky Way galaxy."

Chapter 54: Defending the Galaxy

After lunch, Day Three of the secret agent training camp continued.

"Because of the unprecedented events announced at the intelligence briefing today," said Hot Mustard, "we're accelerating your training so that we can get all of you ready for action." Trevor and Farrah liked the sound of that very much.

"I need a volunteer," said Hot Mustard. Trevor raised his hand, came up to the front, and stood on the mat with Hot Mustard.

"Okay, hit me!" said Hot Mustard, who leaned forward with his hands behind his back. "Right in the face. Don't worry, I won't hit you back."

Trevor had grown used to weird requests like this, so he drew his hand back and aimed right for Hot Mustard's face. "Okay, you asked for it!" said Trevor. Trevor threw his punch, but Hot Mustard leaned to his left, avoiding the punch. Trevor threw another punch, but missed again. Trevor threw two more punches, missing again and again. Hot Mustard always seemed to know which way to lean to avoid getting hit. The whole time Hot Mustard never even moved his feet.

"Wow!" said Trevor. "Impressive!"

Hot Mustard pulled a blindfold out of his pocket and wrapped it around his head, covering his eyes. Everyone was wondering what was up. "Okay, now hit me!"

Trevor felt weird about hitting a guy in the face who was blindfolded, but he figured if anyone could take a punch, it would be Hot Mustard. Trevor wound up again, and threw a hard punch. Hot Mustard leaned to the right, causing Trevor to miss. Trevor tried again, and again, and again but, just like before, could not land a punch.

"How did you do that?" asked Trevor, as Hot Mustard removed his blindfold.

"What I have just shown you," said Hot Mustard, "is how to use Juicy Juicy to win every conflict. The key to hand-to-hand combat is knowing what your opponent is going to do before they do. This is also the key to defending the galaxy from invaders like the Murkians."

"Have the Murkians ever attacked Fruit Smoothie?" asked Trevor.

"Well, they tried once, ten million years ago," said Hot Mustard. "They assembled their battleships and flew into our galaxy, violating every treaty we had ever made with them." Hot Mustard smiled. "Big mistake!"

"What did you do?" asked Farrah.

"Well, it was way before my time," said Hot Mustard, "but we knew they were coming, so they never had a chance. We sent their entire armada forward in time, 100 trillion years, after disabling all of their time traveling technology. They never returned."

"Can you teach us to use our Juicy Juicy to avoid punches, too?" asked Trevor.

"Absolutely. Everyone grab a partner and a blindfold, and let's start practicing. But nobody punch anybody!" said Hot Mustard. "That's only for experts like me!"

The class spent the next hour doing a hand slapping exercise. One person would be blindfolded, with their hands out, palms up. The other person would start with their hands behind their own back, and then try to slap the blindfolded person's hands.

"Use your Juicy Juicy," said Hot Mustard. "Think to yourself, 'I don't want my hands slapped,' and your Juicy Juicy will tell you what to do."

By the end of the hour, everyone had learned how to pull their hands away at exactly the right time to avoid getting slapped. "Awesome!" thought Trevor to himself.

Chapter 55: Mind Reading

As they were waiting for the next class to begin, Trevor raised his hand. He had a question for Hot Mustard. "Right before we fought yesterday," said Trevor, "it felt like you were trying to read my mind. Was that real?"

"Yes it was," said Hot Mustard. "I was trying to figure out what you were going to do once I attacked. Unfortunately for me, I was unsuccessful. I'm not as good at mind reading as Sweet Chili."

Sweet Chili walked up. "Alright class," she said, "it's time that I taught you all how to read minds." Everyone paid close attention. Farrah liked Sweet Chili a lot. They were becoming good friends.

"First of all," said Sweet Chili, "we are all born with the ability to read minds a little bit. Every time you sympathize with a friend, or worry about how someone else feels, you are putting yourself in their place and imagining what they are feeling. Fundamentally, this is the first step to reading someone's mind."

Farrah raise her hand. "So you have to care about the other person?" she asked.

"On some level, yes," said Sweet Chili. "The next step is to use your Juicy Juicy. Ask yourself what the chances are that this person is thinking about feelings, and then about other things, until finally you guess the right thing. Then try to get more specific, like what they might be feeling. Your Juicy Juicy will allow you to narrow down the possibilities. Once you learn to do this quickly, it will be like you are reading their mind."

Trevor remembered how he had used Juicy Juicy to find Farrah while playing hide and seek at Banana's house. "So, it's like a game of hide and seek, but inside someone else's mind?"

"Indeed," said Sweet Chili. "And just like a game of hide and seek, you must be open to every possibility."

"We'll begin with a simple exercise," said Sweet Chili. "Trevor, you think of a number between one and ten. Farrah, I want you to use your Juicy Juicy to guess his number."

Farrah thought to herself. She wondered if Trevor's number was greater than five. Her Juicy Juicy told her it was. Then she wondered if Trevor's number was greater than eight. Her Juicy Juicy told her it was not. Then Farrah wondered if Trevor's number was seven, and her Juicy Juicy told her it was. "Is your number seven?" asked Farrah.

"It is!" exclaimed Trevor. "Wow, Farrah, you can read minds!"

The class paired up into teams again and practiced this exercise for the rest of the day. Everyone became very good at guessing each other's numbers.

When the class was almost over, Farrah asked Sweet Chili a question. "How do you speak to people, inside their heads? Can you teach us how to do this?"

"The trick," said Sweet Chili, "is making it easy for the other person to read your mind. If you make it easy enough, then to them it sounds like you are talking inside their head."

"Whoa!" said Trevor. "I want to learn how to do that!"

"Me too!" said Farrah, inside Trevor's head. "Me too!"

Chapter 56: Set a Great Example

"Farrah, you just spoke to me inside my head!" said Trevor. "You said 'Me too! Me too!' to me." Farrah looked surprised.

"Sweet Chili!" said Farrah, "I did it! I talked to Trevor using my mind!"

"Wow!" said Sweet Chili, "You're a natural. I couldn't do that until I was twice your age!"

Farrah tried it with another friend, but couldn't get it to work. Then she tried it with Trevor again, and it worked, over and over again. "Why can I only talk to Trevor?" asked Farrah.

"Well, remember the trick, Farrah?" said Sweet Chili. "What's really going on is that Trevor is reading your mind. My guess is that Trevor is very good at mind reading because he is a very good listener." With that, the class ended. "See everyone tomorrow," said Sweet Chili.

Trevor and Farrah practiced talking to each other using their minds as they were leaving class to meet up with Professor Sparks and Banana Splash. As they exited the building, Trevor pushed the button on his remote control, causing his time machine to appear.

"By the way," said Banana, "your friend Tommy back on Earth won't remember anything about aliens or wormholes. We had to erase those memories for security reasons. But he will remember all of the good training we gave him, and that you are doing something really important for the good of everyone. It's for the best, really."

"Okay," said Trevor. He figured the Fruit Smoothians knew what they were doing.

"One more thing," said Banana to the group. "We went back in time to try to figure out who gave the free will bomb to those three alien terrorists. Sure enough, it was a secret agent from the planet Murkos. We'll keep you posted as things develop."

Trevor and Farrah returned to their home realities, as was their routine, in Trevor's time machine. After he got home, Trevor remembered his promise to himself to do an extra good job on his homework instead of watching TV. He decided not to watch TV anymore, because he simply didn't have time. When he wasn't working on homework, he practiced his mind reading skills on everyone around him, including his parents, his brother Roo, and his sister Farrah.

The next day at school, which was Thursday, Trevor saw Tommy playing outside during recess. Instead of harassing second and third graders, though, Tommy was playing with them, like a big brother, and making them feel good. When Tommy saw Trevor, he ran over to say hi.

"Hi, Trevor!" said Tommy. "Hey, guess what." Tommy tugged at the collar of his pajamas coming out of the neck hole of his shirt. "I'm wearing my pajamas to school, too!"

"Cool!" said Trevor. Trevor realized he couldn't tell anyone the real reason he was wearing his pajamas, so he made one up. "I really like how comfortable they are! I'm never taking off my pajamas!"

"Me, either!" said Tommy. "Okay, got to go. I want to get to class early so that I can get started on the assignments before anyone else. For some reason," said Tommy, who paused for a deep thought, "I have this strong desire to learn as much as I can and to be the best person I can be, just like you. It feels great! I don't know why, but somehow I feel like I owe this all to you."

"No, you get all of the credit, Tommy," said Trevor. "Keep up the hard work! And way to set a great example for the other kids!"

Chapter 60: The President of the United States

Trevor's next class was math. He had already mastered all of the math assignments from class, so Mrs. Newton gave him a large stack of extra worksheets to do. The harder Trevor worked, the easier math became for him.

After math class, Trevor's class headed to lunch in the cafeteria. Trevor's mom made him a peanut butter and jelly sandwich. He also had a bag of grapes and a bag of carrots. "I'm going to tell my mom to make me the same lunch as you," said one of Trevor's friends from class. "Maybe this way I'll be as smart at math as you."

Trevor realized that his friend wasn't joking. "It's not what I eat for lunch," said Trevor. "It's hard work and practice. The trick is to have fun learning math and other things. Then you'll want to do it all of the time."

"But I just can't do math," said his friend. "I'm not good at it."

"Baloney," said Trevor. "You just need someone to help you. Then with lots of practice, you can be great at math too." Trevor thought up an idea. "Do this. Start working on math problems from class all of the time, instead of watching TV at home. Think of them as puzzles that you want to solve. Each time you solve a problem, celebrate a little bit. Make it a game. Even if it's not fun at first, pretend that you like it."

"Pretend that I like math?" said Trevor's friend.

"Yes," said Trevor. "Pretend that you love math, like it's your favorite thing to do. Then you'll do it all of the time and get really good at it. Just ask your parents and your teachers for help, when you need it. I'll even talk math with you, and in turn you can explain math to younger kids as well. Next thing you know, you'll be proud of how great you're doing, and you'll start to really have fun. You really will love math."

Trevor's friend cracked a big smile. "I'm going to get started right now!" he said, as he ran back to class, earlier than everyone else.

Across the room, Trevor noticed that Tommy was in an argument with a bunch of eighth graders. Tommy was telling them something very passionately. The eighth graders walked over to Trevor's table, and looked at him sternly.

"Tommy says that you are the coolest kid in the school," said Donovan, an eighth grader who was nearly six feet tall. "All I see is a dorky kid wearing his pajamas!"

Trevor laughed. "What does that even mean?" said Trevor. "Who cares who's cool? That's silly! You do your thing, and I'll do mine."

"That's what I thought," said Donovan. "Just another stupid fifth grader."

Just then, a military grade helicopter landed outside the cafeteria windows on the grassy lawn. Three men in suits and sunglasses got out of the helicopter. As they entered the school, they showed their US Secret Service badges to the teachers on lunch duty and asked them some questions. The teachers then pointed at Trevor.

The men in suits walked over to Trevor. Everyone in the cafeteria stopped what they were doing to listen to what was happening. "Are you Trevor?" asked the man in charge.

"Yes," said Trevor. "What's all of this about?"

"We need you to come with us," said the man in charge. "It's a matter of national security."

"What?" asked Trevor.

"National security," said the man in charge. "The President of the United States needs to see you, right away."

Chapter 61: Coolest Kid Ever

Trevor was stunned, but couldn't help making one last comment to Donovan. "Well, gotta go. The President's waiting."

Trevor left his lunch on the table and walked through the cafeteria with the agents. Everyone in the cafeteria was staring at him. Trevor could read all of their minds thinking how cool he was.

"I still think he's a dork," said Donovan. Tommy looked at Donovan and shook his head.

Trevor then turned his attention to the secret agents, but was having a hard time reading their minds. The more he probed, the more they didn't even seem human.

As Trevor and the agents made their way outside, Trevor looked one of the agents in the eye. For a moment, the agent's eye flickered and looked like a cat's eye, or maybe a lizard's. Then suddenly Trevor read one of the agents' minds. "Murkians!" thought Trevor to himself. "They're here to kidnap me!"

Trevor used his martial arts training to drop to the ground and roll away from the Murkians. "Leave the planet Earth, and don't ever come back!" said Trevor.

The Murkians started circling Trevor. As they did, they turned off their cloaking devices and revealed their true forms, which resembled slimy frogs walking on two feet. Everyone in the cafeteria gasped as they crowded around the windows to watch the drama outside.

Before Trevor could shoot a wormhole from his homologizer, two Murkians tried to grab Trevor's arms. Instead, Trevor grabbed their arms and, using his pajamas, pulled the Murkians together with a tremendous force. The two Murkians' heads hit, knocking them unconscious. Then the other Murkian charged and dove at Trevor, who quickly stepped to the side. Trevor's attacker crashed into a metal pole, knocking that Murkian unconscious, too.

The pilot of the helicopter, seeing all of this, tried to make a run for it. He revealed his true form and ran away from Trevor very awkwardly, as a frog might, but as fast as he could. Trevor felt sorry for the guy, but shot him with a wormhole from his homologizer anyway, from fifty yards away.

Trevor then pulled out his walkie talkie. "Code Red! Code Red! Four Murkians on the planet Earth. I repeat, at least four Murkians on the planet Earth. We need to lock it down!" Immediately dozens of Fruit Smoothians, disguised as local policemen, came running from around every corner. Some of them dragged the unconscious Murkians away, and another flew away in the helicopter. The one in charge reported the "all clear" to Trevor, saluted, and then ran off. Within a minute, everything was quiet again, and all of the aliens were gone.

Trevor calmly walked back inside the cafeteria, sat down at his seat, and resumed eating his lunch. At first everyone was quiet, shocked at what they had just seen. Then everyone started crowding around Trevor, including several eighth grade girls, who sat next to him. The crowd started chanting, "Trevor! Trevor! Trevor!"

"Trevor's the coolest kid ever!" said Donovan loudly, so that everyone could hear.

"And he's kind of cute, too!" said one of the girls.

Chapter 62: Don't be a Cheater

Mrs. Newton walked into the lunch room. "Everyone, everyone," she said. "May I have your attention?" Everyone looked up at Mrs. Newton. A blinding light filled the room, stunning everyone for a second.

"Alright, see you Trevor," said the girls, competing for his attention. Everyone else got up too, and returned to their original seats in the cafeteria. Everyone resumed their school day, as if nothing had happened.

Mrs. Newton motioned to Trevor to come on over. He threw away his lunch and walked back to class with her. "Great job, Trevor!" said Mrs. Newton. "You really saved the day. We Fruit Smoothians will be forever grateful for what you are doing for us!"

Trevor was shocked. "You're a Fruit Smoothian?" said Trevor.

"Yes, sorry to surprise you like this, but you are far too important to us for us not to give you some level of security." She paused. "I hope you don't mind, but I had to erase everyone's memory of the alien attack that just happened. The other students will still think you are amazing, by the way." She smiled. "They just won't remember why."

"What about my family?" asked Trevor. "Are they safe?"

"Absolutely," said Mrs. Newton. "Don't worry about a thing. The safest place for your family is right where they are. Farrah and Roo have a different lunch period and are fine, as are your parents. We've secured the Earth with a squadron of battle cruisers, and we have secret agents in key locations. The Murkians may have caught us with our pants down this time, but we won't let that happen again."

"What about me?" said Trevor. "What should I do?"

"Master Lettuce Wraps wants you to keep to the usual schedule," replied Mrs. Newton. "It was your training that saved you this time, and it will be your training that saves you next time, too."

Trevor felt reassured by Mrs. Newton's words, but remained shaken by the day's events. Aliens taking over the Earth never seemed so real. Plus, he had a test coming up.

For the first time in Trevor's life, he noticed it was hard to focus on studying. As he prepared for his grammar exam, he kept drifting off and thinking about the Murkian threat. "One thing at a time," thought Trevor to himself. "Focus on your schoolwork." Trevor settled down and got back to work.

Before the exam, in an effort to be popular with Trevor, one of Trevor's fifth grade friends in another class offered to let Trevor cheat on the exam. "Mrs. Smart uses the same tests in my class as yours," said Trevor's friend. "I already took the test. I can tell you the answers, if you want."

"No way!" said Trevor. "That's cheating! I'm never going to cheat in school. Being honest is much more important than grades." Trevor learned this from his dad.

Trevor's friend looked embarrassed. "Yeah, I was just joking," said his friend. "I'm never going to cheat in school either!"

Chapter 63: Understand Your Feelings

After school, Trevor got into his time machine and picked up Farrah on his way back to Fruit Smoothie, ten thousand years in the future. They arrived one second after they had left, just outside District Headquarters, where Professor Sparks and Banana Splash were still standing.

Farrah heard all about the day's events from Trevor. She had wondered why the other Trevor was being so secretive, and what all the increased security was about. "We share intelligence with ourselves in as many of the other realities as we can," said Banana Splash. "That's one of the technological advantages that we have over the Murkians."

Professor Sparks was alarmed by the recent events. "If anything happens to the planet Earth, I'll feel responsible," he said. "Maybe I never should have invented my time machine."

"That's nonsense," said Banana, as they all walked to Banana's home, together. "The Murkians were already a threat to the Earth. In fact, you're helping to save the Earth."

"I know you're right, logically," said the professor, "but feelings aren't always logical."

"True. That is part of being human," said Banana. "Some of your emotions are out of date, hard wired into your brains from when you were furry little critters, two hundred million years ago. The furry little critters with certain emotions, like fear, survived more often than the furry little critters without these emotions, until finally those were the only furry little critters left. Eventually, after millions of years of natural selection, those furry little critters became you, human beings."

Trevor understood some of what Banana said. In school, Trevor had learned that all life on Earth descended from one celled organisms in the oceans, long ago. Over billions of years, life better suited to the environment reproduced in greater numbers. This process, called natural selection, created wide varieties of species, including fish. Some of the fish evolved into animals that could walk on land. Some of those animals evolved into furry little critters, and then monkeys, and then human beings.

"I see," said Professor Sparks. "I knew animals had feelings, but I never considered the idea that their emotions and my emotions are quite similar."

"Sure they are," said Banana Splash. "Emotions are mostly good for you. You should love your family, and you should be afraid of things that can hurt you. Even furry little critters know this. The problem is when you let your emotions cause you to act like a furry little critter. Your emotions aren't always right. Be a man, not a mouse."

Farrah interrupted. "Like a deer, who freezes when it senses danger. Most of the time this is good for the deer, since being still makes it harder for predators to see the deer."

"Except when the deer freezes in the middle of the road, and a car is coming!" said Trevor. His parents were constantly looking out for deer when they drove their car at night.

"Scared people can freeze up too," said Banana, "which often is not the right decision. We Fruit Smoothians, on the other hand, evolved from animals that were similar to bears on the planet Earth. To this day, we still love to eat nuts and berries."

Professor Sparks smiled. "Wow, Banana!" he said. "You are full of insights today, aren't you? I never thought of my feelings like that before."

"Don't ignore your feelings," said Banana. "Understand them - why they exist, how they are good, and how they are bad. Then use logic and reason, as best you can, to do the right thing."

Chapter 64: The Medal of the Order of the Fruit Smoothians

Trevor and Farrah went to bed at 8:30 p.m. at Banana's house so that they could get a really great night's sleep. They both slept ten and a half hours. Professor Sparks was impressed.

"Sleep is very important," said the professor. "People who get too little sleep don't learn as well as everyone else. And when you work extra hard, you need extra sleep. Sleep is good for your brain, which is doing all kinds of important things while you sleep."

"How much is the right amount of sleep?" asked Trevor.

"That can change from day to day, and it's different for each person. If you wake up without an alarm clock feeling refreshed, and can go the whole day without getting tired, then you're doing it right," said the professor. "You'll be smarter all day long."

Trevor knew some kids in school who always seemed tired. He felt sorry for them since they couldn't think as clearly as he could. Sometimes, especially in the afternoons, they could barely hold their eyes open, much less figure out a hard math problem.

"Also, try thinking about what you've learned each day as you go to sleep," said the professor. "This will help you remember what you've learned each day for a long time - some of it for the rest of your life. Also, if you go to sleep thinking about a math problem, every once in a while you may even wake up with the answer. This works for other kinds of problems too."

"Cool!" said Farrah.

Day Four of the secret agent training camp began with another intelligence briefing. Everyone from the previous day was in attendance. Master Lettuce Wraps led the meeting.

"Banana Splash and his team verified our suspicions that the Murkians were behind the free will bomb that almost exploded at the Café Mobius four days ago," said Master Wraps. "Even worse, the Murkians tried to kidnap Trevor at school in his reality. They must know what we know - that there is a 50% chance that Trevor will save Fruit Smoothie." Master Wraps looked at everyone very seriously.

"The only good news is how well Trevor did at fighting off the Murkians at his school," announced Master Wraps, as he began to clap his hands. "Nice job, Trevor!" Everyone else clapped too. Master Wraps motioned for Trevor to come to the front.

"By your actions, Trevor, you distinguished yourself as one of our finest secret agents. You used your training and instincts to correctly handle a tricky situation that got by all of our other security measures," said Master Wraps. "For your heroism and quick thinking under pressure, I am awarding you the Medal of the Order of the Fruit Smoothians." He then pinned the medal on Trevor, shook Trevor's hand, and motioned for Trevor to sit down.

Farrah clapped for Trevor's award. "I'm glad they didn't try to kidnap me," thought Farrah, "but I sure would like to win a medal!" Sweet Chili smiled at Farrah.

"Unfortunately," said Master Wraps, "we don't have time to celebrate the occasion. Our interrogation of the Murkians that Trevor captured hasn't revealed much we didn't already know. They do, however," he paused, "want to talk to Trevor."

"What do they want to talk to me for?" asked Trevor.

"They wouldn't say," said Master Wraps. "Frankly, I hesitate even asking you for this favor, Trevor, after all you've been through. But we would like to know what they have to say to you. Maybe we can get some useful information."

"I'll do my best," said Trevor. "And thank you for the medal!"

Chapter 65: Power and Freedom

Trevor, Farrah, and Professor Sparks went down to level B686 to talk with the captured Murkians. The Fruit Smoothians left the room hoping this would encourage the Murkians to talk more freely. The Murkians were completely disarmed and in handcuffs and leg cuffs. They looked broken and pathetic, slouching in their prison cells like nothing mattered.

"We just want to talk to Trevor," said the head Murkian with a gritty deep voice.

"No," said Trevor. "Anything you have to say to me you can say in front of my sister Farrah and my brother Professor Sparks. We're a team."

"Well, isn't that nice," said the head Murkian. "I'm touched, really I am. I have three kids of my own." Trevor read his mind and could tell he was lying. He didn't have any kids at all.

"What did you want to say to me?" asked Trevor.

"Well, first of all, Trevor," said the head Murkian, "I'm sorry we got off on the wrong foot. We didn't mean to scare you. In fact, we want to be your friends."

"Then stay away from the planet Earth!" said Farrah.

"Deal," said the head Murkian. "We just have one small little favor to ask of you, Trevor. Don't save the Fruit Smoothians. When the time comes, just go home and stay out of it. It's really none of your business, anyway."

Trevor, Farrah, and Professor Sparks knew that there was no way to trust the Murkians. After they took over Fruit Smoothie, they'd take over Earth too, as soon as they felt like it. Still, they wanted to get more information out of the Murkian prisoners.

"And," continued the head Murkian, "we'll give you whatever you want. Want a trillion dollars? It's yours! Or how about power? We can detonate free will bombs on the planet Earth and give you power over everyone on the planet. No more homework for you!"

Trevor, Farrah, and Professor Sparks were shocked at what they were hearing.

"Or even better," said the head Murkian, "we can make you one of our district governors in charge of a hundred planets in the Milky Way galaxy – you pick the district. It's a big galaxy, you know. Oh, how I would like to be you, Trevor!"

Trevor tried to imagine what it would be like to be in charge of a hundred planets and started to understand the corrupting influence of power. He realized that if he went down that path, he'd end up just like the Murkian he was talking too.

"You know," said the head Murkian, "people need to be controlled. Look at all of the war and violence on your planet, Trevor. Just think how much better things would be if you were in charge. We'll make the Milky Way galaxy a better place together, Trevor. That's all we want to do with our free will bombs – to make the world a better place."

Trevor couldn't stand it anymore. "Controlling people is not making the world a better place!" said Trevor, "Good people are people who choose to make the world a better place. Without freedoms and choices, you stifle good people and any chance at a good society."

"Well, you think about it," said the head Murkian.

"There's nothing to think about," said Trevor. "I'm going to do whatever I can to stop you and the rest of you evil Murkians!"

Chapter 66: Practice Makes Perfect

Trevor, Farrah, and Professor Sparks told the Fruit Smoothians what the Murkian prisoners had said. The information they gathered was very valuable indeed.

"This confirms our worst fears," said Master Wraps. "These free will bombs sound as powerful as we had thought and the Murkians appear to have many of them. An attack on the Milky Way galaxy seems inevitable."

"Are you going to attack Murkos?" asked Trevor.

"Well, there's a problem with that," said Master Wraps. "The Murkians are on every planet in the Andromeda galaxy, and we have no idea where these free will bombs are. We can't destroy an entire galaxy. I wouldn't even do that if we could."

"We're lucky to have you protecting our galaxy," said Trevor. "Thank you so much."

"You're welcome," said Master Wraps. "Now back to class. Your training is the most important thing right now."

Day Four of the secret agent training camp began with more mind reading practice followed by more Juicy Juicy exercises similar to those on Day Three. "We've given you all of your basic skills," said Sweet Chili. "Now it's all about practice."

"Sweet Chili," said Farrah, "what if a free will bomb goes off and neutralizes all of our Juicy Juicy powers? What will we do then?"

Sweet Chili thought about this a bit. "Well, we would be in uncharted waters, my dear. We would have to put our faith in good people to rise to the challenge and set things right. I hope it doesn't come to that, but I'm afraid it might."

Trevor thought some more about the Murkian's offer to make him the ruler of Earth. It troubled him that, deep down inside, there was a small part of him that was intrigued by this. "Controlling people is not nice," thought Trevor. "I would hate it very quickly."

"Indeed you would," said Sweet Chili, inside Trevor's mind, as she gave him a knowing glance. "True happiness comes from people freely choosing to appreciate you, or to love you. This is the wise path." Trevor appreciated Sweet Chili a lot. "I appreciate you too," said Sweet Chili in his mind.

Hot Mustard came over to Trevor. "Trevor, there's one other thing you've got going for you that came in pretty handy at your school," he said, "and it's pretty awesome."

"What's that?" asked Trevor.

"You're a fifth grader," said Hot Mustard, "and a very nice one at that. No one thinks a fifth grader is going to beat up three Murkian secret agents and shoot a fourth one with a wormhole from his homologizer." Hot Mustard chuckled. "They never saw that coming. If I were you, I'd keep my powers hidden as much as possible. With any luck, maybe the Murkians will continue to underestimate you."

"Good idea," said Trevor. "I'll try to blend in at school – just be another student. With any luck, I'll get lost in the crowd."

Chapter 100: Celebrity

The next day, Trevor, Farrah, and Roo got dropped off at school by their mom. It was Friday, Trevor's favorite day of the week. He liked school, but looking forward to the weekend was fun too. "Have a great day!" said their mom, as she drove away. As the three of them approached the school, Trevor noticed that nearly half of the students were wearing pajamas under their clothes. Even the eighth graders were doing it.

"Trevor!" said a sixth grader. "What's up, dude!" The sixth grader put up his hand waiting for Trevor to give him a high five. Five other students did the same thing. Older girls were looking straight at him, which was new, and then walking up to him to say "Hi, Trevor." Boys and girls were crowding around Trevor so much, he could barely get to class.

Farrah and Roo entered the school with Trevor but were pushed to the side by the crowd. "Why does everyone like my dorky brother so much?" thought Farrah to herself. Trevor, who read her mind, tried not to take offense.

"Hey, everyone, this is my sister Farrah and my brother Roo," said Trevor. Suddenly Farrah and Roo were getting mobbed by people saying hi to them as well.

"I'm going to wear my pajamas under my clothes to school tomorrow, too!" thought Roo, who was in kindergarten. "This is cool!"

"Well, so much for blending in," thought Trevor. "So this is what it's like to be a celebrity."

Trevor couldn't help but notice that some of the teachers were staring at him too, wondering what all of the hubbub was about. "He must be a pretty cool kid," thought one of the eighth grade teachers as Trevor walked by.

Once Trevor got to class, he started studying as hard as he could, even before class officially began. He noticed that all of the other fifth graders were studying hard too, just like him. He read their minds. "Maybe if I study hard like Trevor, I'll be popular too." Trevor smiled.

A fifth grade girl walked by Trevor's desk and placed a card on his desk inviting him to her birthday party. Trevor hadn't ever been invited to a girl's birthday party before. "Will you come, please?" asked the fifth grade girl. "We're going to have a pony."

As Trevor answered, he noticed that all of the other girls in the class seemed very interested in his reply. "Can my sister Farrah come too? She's in the fourth grade," said Trevor. She nodded her head yes. "Okay, I'll ask my mom," said Trevor.

Suddenly, Trevor could read the minds of all of the other girls in the class. "I'm definitely going to that party, too." The girls who hadn't already been invited were thinking about how they could get invited. A couple of the girls were thinking how they could become friends with Trevor's sister, just so they could be invited over to Trevor's house sometime.

With all of the distractions, Trevor was having a hard time focusing on his work. "I'll just keep working hard," thought Trevor to himself. "Eventually, people will forget about me, and things will go back to normal. Then I'll blend in again. Just another student in the crowd."

Chapter 101: Farrah's Surprise

After school, Trevor got into his time machine and picked up Farrah from her reality on his way back to Fruit Smoothie, ten thousand years in the future. As usual, Professor Sparks and Banana Splash were waiting for them. They all walked back to Banana's house together.

"Tomorrow, we've got an extra special surprise for you, Farrah," said Banana Splash. Farrah spent the rest of the day wondering what it might be, and the rest of the night dreaming about it.

The next morning, Banana Splash told everyone what the surprise was. "Today, the four of us are going to take our training camp on the road," said Banana. "We're going to go get Farrah's unicorn!"

"A flying unicorn," said Farrah excitedly, "who can talk, read minds, and grant wishes?"

"More or less," said Banana. "You may have to compromise on a few things."

Trevor, Farrah, Professor Sparks, and Banana Splash all got into Trevor's time machine. Trevor told Jeeves to take them wherever Banana said to go.

"Jeeves, take us to the planet Mystica, in the Whirlpool Galaxy, one billion years in the past," said Banana. Farrah was so excited she could barely stand it. Trevor was very curious, but otherwise wasn't sure why anyone would want a unicorn.

"In many cultures, on many different planets, the idea of a magical horse has symbolized pure goodness and innocence," said Banana Splash. "On one planet, the planet Mystica, a highly advanced civilization, inspired by this idea, bio-engineered the most amazing horse ever."

Trevor's time machine raced through the cosmos and approached the Whirlpool Galaxy, the most beautiful galaxy he had ever seen. Everyone paused to take in its beauty and grandeur.

Banana continued. "In the same way that humans have bred dogs for thousands of years to serve a wide variety of purposes, the Mysticans bred horses, but for billions of years, and with advanced technology. They even bred a horse that could fly."

"Wow," said Farrah.

"Of course it's a very tiny horse," said Banana Splash, "there's no way a full sized horse could fly. That would be ridiculous." Banana laughed, but stopped when he saw that Farrah wasn't laughing with him.

"Will she have a horn?" asked Farrah.

"Oh, yes," said Banana. "And they have fluffy tails and are as cute as they can be."

"Okay, I guess," said Farrah, who was a little disappointed about not being able to ride her unicorn because of its small size. "Can she talk?"

"Oh, yes, and read minds," said Banana. "The Mysticans bred these horses to be very intelligent and very wise. In fact," said Banana, "these horses are among the wisest life forms we have ever encountered. They are quite remarkable."

"Can they grant wishes?" asked Farrah. Farrah held her breath for the answer.

"Sure," said Banana, "they can grant wishes, here and there." He paused. "Just like we can all grant wishes, here and there. But they aren't technically magical, though."

"Awww," said Farrah.

"Still," said Banana, "they do have a way of bringing out the best in people. It is hard to do anything wrong around a unicorn, a life form so good and innocent that all they want to do is help other people. In this way, there is something quite magical about them."

Chapter 102: Rainbow

Trevor's time machine landed on the planet Mystica in a grassy field surrounded by snowcapped mountains.

"One more thing," said Banana, "You can't own a unicorn, any more than you can own another person. Also, these are highly intelligent life forms. In fact, they are smarter than us in many ways. They get offended when people call them pets or try to buy one of them. So be nice."

Everyone exited Trevor's time machine and saw that they were surrounded by dozens of small unicorns with wings, each about the size of a large dog. The unicorns were mostly white, but with different colored manes and tails. Some were blue, pink, purple, white, yellow, and green, and some were several colors. One of them, whose mane and tail had every color of the rainbow, stood out to Farrah.

"Oh, they are adorable!" said Farrah, who fell in love with them instantly.

The rainbow colored one walked over to Farrah. "You smell very sweet," she said.

"Thank you," said Farrah, "it is very nice to meet you. My name is Farrah. What's your name?"

"Rainbow," said the unicorn.

"Wow!" said Farrah, "What a coincidence. I was hoping your name was Rainbow!"

"Yes, I know," said the unicorn. "That's why I chose it." Farrah was confused at first, but then remembered that these unicorns could read minds.

"I've always wanted to be friends with a flying unicorn who could talk, read minds, and grant wishes," said Farrah. "We could go on adventures together, help people who needed help, tell stories, and have all kinds of fun. Would you be my friend?"

"Sure," said Rainbow. "I would love to be your friend. I'll even help you stop those evil Murkians who are trying to take over the Milky Way galaxy."

"Wow!" said Farrah, "You can read me like a book, can't you?"

"Yes," said Rainbow, "which is why I like you. You have a pure heart."

Farrah was the happiest she had ever been. "I love you, Rainbow!"

"When you need me, just think of me," said Rainbow, "and I will come right away."

"But how will you find me?" asked Farrah. "We live in different galaxies."

"Oh, I can create wormholes with my mind. When you think of me, I'll be there."

Farrah was thrilled. "Wow!"

"In fact," said Rainbow, "would you like me to give you a ride back to Fruit Smoothie?"

"Yes I would!" said Farrah.

With that, a wormhole, very similar to the arches on Fruit Smoothie, opened up. Everyone walked through the wormhole to find themselves back on Fruit Smoothie, one second after they had left Banana's house. Trevor pushed the button on his time machine and was relieved that it reappeared at Banana's house too. He didn't want to lose it.

"Rainbow, have we met before?" asked Trevor, who thought he recognized Rainbow from his dream Sunday morning.

Rainbow shook her head no. "You're the first humans I've ever met. It is so nice to meet you!"

Farrah spent the rest of the day getting to know Rainbow, who was just as excited about being friends with Farrah as Farrah was about being friends with Rainbow. They were a perfect match. Trevor was happy to see Farrah so happy.

"Best day ever!" said Farrah.

Chapter 103: Pure Genius

The next two weeks were both busy and exciting. Trevor and Farrah completed their official training and became full-fledged secret agents, all while doing excellent work in school. Farrah was spending a lot of time with Rainbow and Sweet Chili and was getting very good at reading minds, just like Trevor. Trevor was spending extra time with Banana Splash, who was sharing some of his special talents and knowledge with him.

Professor Sparks and Banana Splash were also keeping an eye on the Murkian threat. Their biggest concern was that everyone's Juicy Juicy was not working as well as it had in the past. Master Lettuce Wraps explained the situation at an intelligence briefing.

"For some reason, our Juicy Juicy is not working properly, especially for predicting events that are far in the future. If this trend continues, we could lose all of our Juicy Juicy skills."

"All of this is consistent with a free will bomb attack coming soon," said Banana Splash. "Our top scientists think that our Juicy Juicy will cease to work inside the blast radius of a free will bomb." Everyone looked very concerned. "Given that people are having problems with their Juicy Juicy everywhere, a free will bomb attack on all of Fruit Smoothie seems likely."

"Does anyone know where the Murkians are holding these free will bombs?" asked Professor Sparks. Trevor and Farrah were wondering the same thing.

"Our secret agents are on every major planet in the Andromeda galaxy trying to figure that out," said Master Wraps. "All we need now is some good luck. So far, though, we've got nothing. It's like the Murkians are always one step ahead of us."

"The other thing we've learned," said Banana Splash, "is more about the nature of a free will bomb. It's not quite as bad as we had thought. Apparently, a free will bomb can't make you do anything that you wouldn't have done without the bomb, on your worst possible day. You're still you, and it will still seem like you have free will, but you won't."

"I see," said Professor Sparks. "The person choosing the future can still only choose among possible futures, futures that might have happened anyway, however improbable."

"So if the Murkians attacked us with free will bombs," said Trevor, "they could choose the future where all of the good luck is on their side and all of the bad luck is on our side, for example. They'd always be at their best, and we'd always be at our worst."

"Exactly," said Banana, "but they can't make a good person do bad things, unless that person might have done those things anyway."

Farrah had an idea. "Maybe free will bombs have already gone off on every planet in the Andromeda galaxy," she suggested. "Maybe that's why the Murkians have always been one step ahead of us, and we can't catch a break. Maybe it's because they are controlling all of the luck in the Andromeda galaxy already."

"That's genius!" said Professor Sparks, "Pure genius!" Banana Splash and Master Wraps agreed, nodding their heads. Trevor was impressed with his sister Farrah, who was always coming up with good ideas.

"The only problem," said Banana, "is that we still have no idea what to do."

Chapter 104: Space and Time

After the meeting, Farrah went off with Sweet Chili and Rainbow to practice her mind reading skills. Trevor and Professor Sparks joined Banana for some advanced skills lessons.

"Banana, how do you stop time?" asked Trevor. "Can I learn how to do that?"

"Probably not," said Banana. "You're either born with this ability or you aren't. Nobody knows why. When I want to stop time, I just do it. Only a few Fruit Smoothians have this ability."

"Can you explain what it's like, from your perspective?" asked Professor Sparks.

"Well, it's kind of like controlling a wormhole with your mind," said Banana, "except that instead of controlling something like a rubber band, it's like I'm controlling spacetime itself."

"What is spacetime?" asked Trevor. Trevor realized this must be a very deep question.

"Space and time are two sides of the same coin," said Banana. "They're different, but not that different."

Professor Sparks explained, "For example, consider a gallon of milk versus a two liter container of soda pop. Clearly milk and soda pop are different, just like space and time are different. Gallons and liters are different too, but not that different, since both measure volume, and you can always convert between the two. Space and time, while different, can be measured with the same units, just like milk and soda pop."

"Really?" said Trevor. "How so?"

"Well," said Professor Sparks. "Just as one gallon is about four liters, we can convert between seconds, a measure of time, and miles, a measure of distance. In fact, one second is about 186,000 miles, or about 300,000 kilometers."

"Really!" said Trevor. He hadn't heard this before.

"Yep," said Banana. "The first person from your planet to realize this was Albert Einstein. We Fruit Smoothians, on the other hand, have known this for billions of years."

Trevor had heard of Einstein, but didn't know his work concerned space and time.

"The unification of space and time into one concept called spacetime is called Special Relativity," said Professor Sparks. "My time traveling technology is based on it, as well as General Relativity, Einstein's even more profound idea."

"What's that?" asked Trevor.

"That matter curves spacetime," said Professor Sparks. "This simple idea is at the heart of understanding the large scale structure of the universe including gravity, black holes, dark energy, and the Big Bang - the event that describes the beginning of time itself."

"Whoa," said Trevor.

"The reason I'm telling you this," said Professor Sparks, "is that curving spacetime, or bending it, if you prefer, is the fundamental idea behind wormholes."

"And stopping time," interrupted Banana. "I'm sure of it."

Chapter 105: Einstein's Happiest Thought

Trevor wanted to learn more, but wasn't sure what question to ask next.

"For example, gravity is explained by the curvature of spacetime," said Professor Sparks. Banana smiled. He loved this stuff.

"Really!" said Trevor. "Are you serious?"

"Absolutely," said Professor Sparks. "I can explain by using an analogy. Imagine a bowling ball that you put on your bed. This bowling ball is very heavy, so it will make a big dimple in your bed. Can you visualize this so far?"

"Sure," said Trevor.

"Okay," said Professor Sparks. "Now suppose I place a bunch of tiny marbles on your bed, all around the bowling ball. What will happen?"

"The marbles will lean against the bowling ball," said Trevor, "because of the dimple in the bed."

"Very good," said Professor Sparks. "Now suppose I lightly flick one of the marbles away from the bowling ball, just a little bit. What happens?"

"The marble goes away from the bowling ball for a second, and then comes back," said Trevor. So far this seemed pretty easy to Trevor.

"Exactly," said Professor Sparks. "Now here's the fun part," he paused for dramatic effect. "In my analogy, the bowling ball represents the Earth, and the marbles represent people on the surface of the Earth. When you lightly flick a marble, this represents a person jumping up and then coming back down to the surface of the Earth."

"Cool," said Trevor. "Makes sense, I guess, since the Earth is round and people live on every side of the Earth." Trevor already knew that "up" means away from the center of the Earth, and that "down" means toward the center of the Earth. "Cool analogy," said Trevor. "But what does this have to do with the curvature of spacetime?"

"Okay, here's the really cool part," said Professor Sparks. Banana was on the edge of his seat, wanting to take in Trevor experiencing one of the coolest ideas ever. "In my analogy, the bed represents spacetime. The bowling ball curves the bed which causes the marbles to press against the bowling ball, right?"

"Sure," said Trevor.

"Similarly," said Professor Sparks, "the Earth curves spacetime which causes people to press against the Earth. We call this effect gravity."

"Hence, 'matter curves spacetime' explains gravity," interrupted Banana.

"Wow," said Trevor, "I think I understood that." Trevor started jumping up and down. "Look, I'm a marble jumping up and down on a bowling ball!"

"Indeed you are!" said Professor Sparks, who laughed. "By the way, Albert Einstein called this idea his happiest thought."

"Einstein must have been really good at math," said Trevor.

"Yes," said Professor Sparks, "but there were plenty of people as good at math as Einstein. What made Einstein one of the greatest thinkers ever was his ability to come up with completely new ideas, like the one we just described. He enjoyed thinking about lots of ideas - some crazy, some good, some wrong, but some brilliant - for long periods of time."

"In other words," said Banana, "he was a dreamer. We should all do that more often."

Chapter 106: Basketball

Trevor and Farrah continued to alternate days between their home realities and Fruit Smoothie, ten thousand years in the future. Trevor enjoyed his time back home very much.

As Trevor took a shower, he drifted away, thinking about his training and how he was getting very good at controlling wormholes with his mind. He was getting so good, in fact, that he could do tricks with wormholes, juggling several at a time. Just then, his mom pulled the curtain back.

"Are you taking a shower in your pajamas?" she exclaimed, bewildered.

"Yes I am," said Trevor. "A little privacy, please?" Trevor pulled the curtain back.

Trevor's mom laughed. "Kids are so funny!" she said out loud to herself, as she walked away.

Trevor's mom didn't know that his pajamas were designed to let soapy water pass right through them, and that they were self-drying. Trevor didn't even need to dry his hair. He did have to brush his teeth, though, which he did after every meal, as well as right after school.

Today was Saturday, though, so Trevor, Farrah, and Roo spent their day playing outside with Alex, Allie, and Aaron. Their favorite game was basketball, which they played in Trevor's driveway. Roo and Aaron were the shortest and only five years old, so when they had the ball, no one was allowed to get in their way or block their shots. Everyone tried their hardest, but also made sure everyone else was having fun too.

Trevor wasn't as good at basketball as his best friend Alex, who was quick and fast and could shoot the ball very well. Trevor could shoot pretty well too, but wasn't nearly as quick and fast as Alex. In the past, sometimes Trevor didn't want to play basketball against Alex because he didn't like to lose.

However, since getting his pajamas, Trevor started playing basketball every chance he got. Trevor saw that if he got discouraged and never played basketball, he wouldn't get any practice. On the other hand, Trevor saw that if he kept trying his best, he would get more and more practice at basketball and would eventually be very good at it.

"I think it's great the way you're trying harder at basketball," said Trevor's dad. "You're going to be a very good basketball player some day!"

Trevor smiled. It also didn't hurt that he always knew where the ball would bounce, because of his pajamas. Trevor was getting most of the rebounds these days. His pajamas also helped him make better decisions, like when to pass the ball or when to try to block a shot.

To get faster, Trevor started doing sprints in his front yard, running from one line in the yard to another as fast as he could. After a quick rest, he would then run back the other way, as fast as he could. He kept doing this until his legs hurt, telling him to stop. Trevor knew that any kid who did sprints like these was going to get very fast and quick.

Trevor also vowed to stop eating so much candy and junk food. He didn't want to get fat. "I'm going to get as strong and healthy as I can," thought Trevor to himself. "Then maybe someday I'll be able to beat Alex at a game of basketball."

Chapter 110: Tricks

At 4 p.m., Trevor went for a short walk around the corner from his house and got into his time machine. He picked up Farrah from her reality and took both of them to Fruit Smoothie, ten thousand years in the future, as usual.

"I've got a pretty cool trick to show you," said Farrah. "My unicorn friend Rainbow granted me my first wish."

"Really?" said Trevor. Trevor was very impressed by Rainbow and liked her a lot.

After walking back to Banana's house with Banana, Trevor, and Professor Sparks, Farrah was ready to show everyone her big trick. She pulled a jump rope out of her purse.

"You're going to jump rope?" asked Trevor. "I thought you were going to do something amazing."

Farrah then started skipping rope really fast, singing a song as she did it. "Cinderella, dressed in yella, went upstairs to kiss a fella. Made a mistake and kissed a snake! How many doctors did it take?" Suddenly, a wormhole opened up where the jump rope had been, and then closed in an instant around Farrah. Farrah was gone.

Five seconds later, everyone heard a whirling sound on the other side of the yard, which sounded like someone jumping rope very fast. Sure enough, it was Farrah.

"Ta da!" yelled Farrah. "It's a wormhole jump rope!"

"That's amazing!" said Trevor. "Even I want to learn how to jump rope now!" Banana and Professor Sparks were very impressed as well.

Trevor spent the next hour learning how to jump rope, and then how to create a wormhole with Farrah's jump rope. "When the rope gets going fast enough, it automatically creates a wormhole that you pass through," said Farrah. "You can go anywhere you like, in the future or the past."

Trevor was happy Farrah had her own way of traveling through time now. But he still liked his time machine more though since he could talk to Jeeves whenever he wanted. Also, he had cup holders.

"I've got a trick to show you too," said Trevor to everyone. Everyone looked at Trevor as he fired three wormholes into the air with the homologizer in his watch and kept them going in a circle above his head. Then he brought the wormholes together to form three linked rings in the air for a few seconds, before letting them shrink down to nothing.

"Awesome!" said Farrah.

"Very cool!" said Professor Sparks.

Banana was taken aback. "Trevor, how did you do that?"

"Is that supposed to be hard?" asked Trevor.

"Trevor, I can't even do that," said Banana, "and I'm one of the best there is. I didn't even think that was possible."

Chapter 111: A Flying Chicken

Farrah was also very impressed with Trevor's trick. It was getting late, so everyone went inside Banana's house for dinner. They always ate dinner together in the grand banquet hall. Banana kept his house looking like the Biltmore Estate, at Farrah's request.

Trevor had gotten into the habit of wishing for healthier food than he did on the first day. He wasn't eating pizza anymore, since eating a lot of cheese is high in saturated fat. He also stopped eating cake, ice cream, and candy. Instead, he liked to eat fish for dinner, especially salmon, with brown rice and vegetables like broccoli and green beans. He ate oatmeal with blueberries on top for breakfast in the mornings. His favorite lunchtime meal was now a bean burrito. He had heard that beans were very good for you. Trevor's favorite snacks were now apples and oranges.

Everyone was in a good mood, telling jokes and laughing a lot.

"Does anyone want Rainbow to grant them a wish?" asked Farrah. "After all," said Farrah, "she likes all of you very much."

"Sure," said Trevor. "I'd like a flying chicken!" Everyone laughed.

"And I'd like a flying wheelchair!" said Professor Sparks. Everyone visualized Professor Sparks flying around in a wheelchair, and laughed.

Suddenly, the whole house started shaking. A very loud noise from outside filled the mansion. The chandelier above the table swayed back and forth. "Murkians!" yelled Banana. "Everyone, stay inside," said Banana. "We'll be safe in here." Loud booming sounds could be heard in the distance.

"Shouldn't we do something?" asked Trevor.

"Yes, we're going to save Fruit Smoothie and the rest of the galaxy," said Banana. "But today, we're going to let the Fruit Smoothian defense forces do their job. Our job is to stay safe, for now." More booming sounds could be heard in the distance, then one that sounded close.

A moment later, a wave passed through Banana's house, distorting space and time. Everyone and everything in Banana's house bobbed up and down, like rubber duckies in a bathtub. Everyone seemed to be fine, but something was different.

"I think we've just been hit by a free will bomb," said Banana. "If I'm right, we do not have any free will right now."

Trevor pulled out his futurometer and asked it a question, but it didn't respond. "My futurometer isn't working," said Trevor.

"That's because all of our Juicy Juicy has been knocked out," said Banana. "All of that great intuition that we're used to having … well, it's gone. All of our decisions from this point on are suspect."

"What about the Murkians?" asked Farrah. "Will they invade now?"

"Maybe," said Banana, "but I doubt it. They already control us. All they have to do now is let us destroy ourselves."

Chapter 112: A Good Night's Sleep

Farrah was scared, so she wished for Rainbow to appear. Rainbow could read minds and so realized what had just happened.

"Stay calm, everyone," said Rainbow. "You are good people. Remember, no one can make you do anything that you wouldn't do otherwise."

"Well, I'm going to have some ice cream," said Trevor, "maybe even two or three bowls."

"Trevor, no!" said Rainbow. "That's the Murkians controlling you. You stopped eating ice cream, remember?"

"Oh, yeah," said Trevor, "you're right!"

"Well, I'm going home to my reality," said Professor Sparks. "I think Trevor and Farrah should go home too."

"Fine, go home!" said Banana. "I always knew you were a coward!"

Professor Sparks was offended. "Well, how do I know if you are even my friend? You just used me to get to Trevor, as I recall!"

Everyone started arguing, except for Rainbow who saw what was going on. A tear fell down Rainbow's cheek.

"Awww," said Farrah. "We're making Rainbow cry!"
Everyone looked at Rainbow and felt ashamed. They realized what
was going on.

"We were having such a wonderful time before the free will
bomb went off," said Banana Splash, "and now we're arguing with
each other. It's the Murkians controlling us!"

"It must be," said Professor Sparks. "I'm sorry for what I said."

"Me too," said Banana. Everyone came together for a group
hug.

"But what do we do now?" asked Trevor.

"I don't know," said Banana, "but I think we should stay up all
night until we figure it out."

Rainbow interrupted. "Murkians controlling you ..."

"Ah," said Professor Sparks, "Normally we'd go to bed and get
a good night's sleep. Anytime we do something different from
normal, we need to assume it's the Murkians trying to control us to
their advantage."

"I see," said Banana. "Then let's all go to sleep and get plenty
of rest. We'll stick to our usual routine as much as we can in order
to minimize the control that the Murkians have on us. That means
we'll report to District Headquarters tomorrow morning, as usual,
and see what's going on."

"Agreed," said Trevor.

"Agreed," said Farrah.

Rainbow smiled. "And I'll stay with you until this threat is
resolved. You are my friends, and I love you all."

Chapter 113: A Great Idea

The next morning, Trevor woke up with a great idea. He often had his best ideas in the morning, right after a good night's sleep. He figured that was why the Murkians tried to stop them from sleeping normally.

Trevor joined everyone at the breakfast table. Rainbow ate her food from a dish on the floor. "Professor Sparks," said Trevor, "since Rainbow wasn't here when the free will bomb went off, does that mean that the Murkians can't control her right now?"

Professor Sparks looked at Banana Splash, thought for a second, and then replied. "Yes … yes, I think you are right." Banana nodded his head in agreement.

"So let's just do whatever Rainbow says," said Trevor. "Banana, you said that unicorns were very wise, and smarter than us, in many ways, right? Let's use this to our advantage."

Everyone thought about Trevor's plan, but no one liked it. Banana laughed, saying that the idea was ridiculous, and Professor Sparks dismissed the idea without saying why. Farrah pretended like she didn't even hear the idea.

"Hello!" said Trevor. "I just came up with a great idea. We need to discuss it."

"Look, Trevor, I like you," said Banana Splash, "but every bone in my body says that your idea is a bad idea. I've got to go with my gut."

"But your gut is being controlled by the Murkians!" said Trevor. "Remember when you taught us about our feelings that we inherited from furry little critters? You told us to understand our feelings, but to use logic and reason in the end. Well, now is the time to use logic and reason, if there ever was a time!"

"That makes sense," said Banana Splash. "Okay, I'll think about your idea." Banana thought about Trevor's proposal and did his best to argue against it. Professor Sparks tried his best too, as did Farrah.

"Hmmm," said Professor Sparks, "this has never happened to me before. My instincts seem to be way off. Your idea makes perfect sense logically, but my gut still hates it."

Farrah agreed. "The Murkians must be choosing futures for us where our instincts are as bad as possible," she said. "We should only use logic and reason from now on."

"Trevor, I am impressed with you," said Banana Splash. "Even on your worst day you could come up with a great idea and have the confidence to stand by it. Bravo!"

Trevor smiled. "Thank you." Everyone started praising Trevor, talking about how smart he was, and how much they appreciated him. This went on for an hour.

"What were we talking about just now?" asked Trevor. "Seems like I had a great idea. Does anyone remember what it was?" Everyone started scratching their heads. Rainbow waited patiently.

"Oh, yeah," said Farrah. "We were all going to agree to do whatever Rainbow says."

"Right," said Trevor. "All agreed?"

"Yes!" said everyone together. They focused on their decision, hoping to remember it later. They knew it would take a lot of discipline to do what Rainbow told them to do, no matter what.

Rainbow spoke up. "You are an impressive group, even after a free will bomb. I will do my best to serve you well."

Chapter 114: A Cute Unicorn

Trevor, Farrah, Professor Sparks, and Banana Splash were behind schedule, but otherwise fine. "I keep losing track of time," said Professor Sparks. "Those evil Murkians are starting to annoy me!"

"Patience, professor," said Rainbow. "You're doing great." The professor nodded.

As the group left Banana's house, Banana suddenly realized that he didn't know how to get to District Headquarters anymore. "I always used my Juicy Juicy to find my way!" said Banana.

"Not to worry," said Farrah. "I wrote down directions on the first day. I can lead the way."

"Well hello, Miss Smarty Pants!" said Trevor. "Look at me, I know everything." Trevor put his hands together above his head and pretended to be a ballerina, spinning around, doing a nice pirouette. Professor Sparks and Banana both laughed.

Farrah started to say something mean back, but then saw Rainbow, with her big eyes, staring at her. Trevor then realized his mistake, and apologized. "Sorry, Farrah," said Trevor. Professor Sparks and Banana apologized too.

By the time the group got to District Headquarters, they were very late. "Where is everyone?" asked Trevor. There weren't any people going in or out of the building. As they walked around level B343, they saw that Master Wraps was the only one on the entire floor.

"Well, it's about time!" said Master Wraps. "I should have you all arrested for dereliction of duty! Do you know what time it is?" He didn't sound like himself.

"What's happening?" asked Banana Splash.

"Mass confusion," said Master Wraps. "The Murkians used free will bombs to take out our outer planetary defenses, allowing their bombers to detonate free will bombs over the entire planet. I'm in the process of ordering a full scale counter attack. If it's war they want, it's war they'll get!"

"Anyone killed?" asked Trevor.

"Oddly, no," said Master Wraps. "No damage anywhere either, except for the free will bombs."

"Why would they?" asked Professor Sparks. "You don't destroy a planet under your control. You use it for something important."

"Well, they don't control me!" said Master Wraps. "We'll see who's in control when I destroy their entire galaxy!"

Trevor knew something wasn't right. "Master Wraps, two weeks ago you told me you would never destroy an entire galaxy, even if you could. I think you are being controlled right now!"

Master Wraps looked very annoyed at Trevor. "Everyone, get out of my office right now, or I'll have you arrested!" He shoved them out, slammed the door behind them, and then continued ordering the attack on the Andromeda galaxy. He was startled when he saw Rainbow standing behind him.

"Well, aren't you a cute unicorn!" said Master Wraps. He stared into her eyes. A tear came to his eye as he thought about all of the innocent people he was about to kill. "Stand down," said Master Wraps, into his microphone. "Return to base. I repeat, return to base. Attack cancelled. I repeat, attack cancelled."

Chapter 115: Ice Cream, Anyone?

Master Wraps let everyone back into his office. "Thank you, everyone, for stopping me from doing something horrific. I can't believe I almost destroyed an entire galaxy."

"That's the power of the free will bombs," said Banana Splash. "We need to stick together, or we'll all be at our worst. In fact, we've all agreed to do whatever Rainbow says. Rainbow is pure of heart, and she was not hit by the free will bombs."

"Nice to meet you, Rainbow," said Master Wraps. "Thank you again." He paused. "Can I join your group? I don't think I should be left by myself. I might do something very bad."

"Sure," said Trevor. "What now?"

"Let's figure this out together," said Master Wraps, "like someone would solve a riddle." He paused. "Whoever is controlling me almost had me destroy the Andromeda galaxy, or at least most of it. Why would they want me to do that?"

"The Murkians are a cruel people," said Banana Splash, "who wouldn't care if we killed everyone else in their galaxy. In fact, they might even prefer it. Since they knew the attack was coming, they were probably in bunkers somewhere, perfectly safe."

"I see," said Master Wraps. "Getting us to do their dirty work. Then they get whoever survives in the Andromeda galaxy to destroy all of the planets in the Milky Way galaxy to get revenge. Everyone ends up dead, except for the Murkians. It's brilliantly evil."

Hot Mustard approached the group. He was very upset. "Master Wraps!" he yelled, in a threatening manner. "Why did you stop the attack? That's treason!"

Master Wraps did not like being yelled at, nor was he scared of Hot Mustard. "Mind your tongue, Hot Mustard, or I'll have you cleaning toilets so fast you won't know the difference between a toilet and your water bowl!"

"I'm reporting you," said Hot Mustard, "to the High Counsel, for treason." Hot Mustard marched off.

"You'll do no such thing," said Master Wraps. "Banana, arrest Hot Mustard. Lock him up downstairs until he calms down."

Hot Mustard turned around, thought for a second, and then laughed. "Agent Banana Splash? Arrest me? What a joke!" He continued marching off, on his way to report Master Wraps.

Banana Splash approached Hot Mustard. "You're under arrest. Lie down on the ground with your hands behind your head." Hot Mustard kept marching off, ignoring Banana. "Buzz off, Banana, if you know what's good for you!" said Hot Mustard.

Banana shot a wormhole at Hot Mustard who used his mind to deflect it. Then Hot Mustard turned and charged Banana.

"Banana time out," said Banana. Hot Mustard froze, with a very angry expression on his face. He was piping hot mad. Everyone else watched as Banana left on the elevator and came back with so much food from the cafeteria he could barely carry it all. He put three ice cream cones in Hot Mustard's pants and pushed an ice cream cake into Hot Mustard's face. "That should cool him off," said Banana.

"Banana time in!" said Banana, as he shot Hot Mustard with a wormhole. Banana stood alone with another ice cream cake that he didn't use. "Ice cream, anyone?"

Chapter 116: Don't Do Drugs

Everyone went down to B686 to talk to Hot Mustard who was in one of the holding cells. When they got there, there were secret agents letting him out of the cell. "Put him back in there!" said Master Wraps. The secret agents obeyed Master Wraps's orders.

The group spent the next hour explaining the day's events to Hot Mustard, who apologized for his actions. Hot Mustard said he understood the logic behind Master Wraps's decision to cancel the attack. "It's just that every part of my being told me an attack was the right thing to do," said Hot Mustard. "It's hard to go against your gut feelings sometimes."

"Eventually, I'll let you out," said Master Wraps, "but for right now, I want to keep you locked up, Hot Mustard. It's for your own good." Hot Mustard nodded in agreement.

"I do have another idea, though, if I may," said Hot Mustard. He was trying to be polite.

"Okay, let's hear it," said Master Wraps.

"We know there's a 50% chance that Trevor will save our planet, right?"

"Yes," said Master Wraps.

"And we want to increase that number to something even higher, like 75%, right?"

"Sure," said Master Wraps.

"Then let's give Trevor some pills which will make him smarter and some shots which will make him stronger. He needs every advantage he can get."

"Sounds like a good idea to me," said Master Wraps. Banana nodded in agreement.

"No," said Trevor. "I won't take any drugs." Farrah and Professor Sparks supported Trevor. They all had the same parents who warned them about the dangers of taking drugs.

"Trevor," said Hot Mustard, "I take these drugs all the time. It's one of the reasons I'm so strong. Trust me, it's good for you."

"No," said Trevor. "I promised my parents I wouldn't ever do drugs. I'm not going to start now. Also, you don't know what the long term effects of these drugs are on you, much less me."

"Trevor," said Master Wraps, "your parents aren't here, and nobody is going to tell them."

"My answer is still no," said Trevor. "I only take drugs when prescribed by a doctor, a licensed human doctor, and even then, we get opinions from multiple doctors sometimes. In the long run, these drugs could seriously hurt me, or even kill me."

"We're your friends," said Banana, "we wouldn't give you drugs that could hurt you."

"But you have no way of knowing," said Trevor, "especially with your Juicy Juicy not working. I think those evil Murkians are trying to get you to hurt me right now. Drugs can destroy people's lives. Some people even destroy their lives with alcohol."

Banana and Master Wraps thought for a second. "Maybe," said Banana. "It is kind of weird how we never suggested this idea before the free will bombs went off." They thought some more, discussing the idea together for a few minutes, off in a corner.

"You're right, Trevor," said Master Wraps. "Having you take drugs would be a stupid and reckless gamble. Nice job standing up to us!"

"Great job, Trevor!" said Farrah.

"Yes, well done, Trevor!" said Professor Sparks.

Chapter 120: Shiny Silver Dollar

Trevor looked at his watch which read 4 p.m. It was time for Trevor and Farrah to return home, at least under normal circumstances.

"Should we keep to our usual schedules?" asked Trevor. "If so, it's time for us to go." Everyone looked to Rainbow for guidance, since she was the only one not being controlled by the Murkians.

"Yes, I think that would be best," said Rainbow. "It's a risk letting you both go off by yourselves, but I think it's the right decision. Just remember: the Murkians are choosing the future for you that favors them the most, but they can't make you into a bad person. Always do what is right and you'll be fine."

Everyone exited the building to see Trevor and Farrah off. They all realized there was a chance that Trevor and Farrah would never come back. "I have faith in them," said Rainbow. "Something tells me that after Trevor and Farrah come back, we'll have a new strategy for dealing with the Murkians."

"Everything in my gut tells me this is a bad idea," said Professor Sparks, with Banana and Master Wraps nodding in agreement, "which is why this is probably a great idea."

Trevor and Farrah got into Trevor's minivan time machine. "Home, Jeeves, for both of us," said Trevor. Farrah got dropped off in her home reality first. Jeeves then returned Trevor to his home reality.

As Trevor approached his house, he could see everyone still playing outside. He reminded himself not to burden anyone else with the entire galaxy being in danger, ten thousand years in the future. "That is a very long time from now," thought Trevor. "Why do I even care? I should enjoy being a kid today. I'm going to have some fun!"

Trevor pulled out his futurometer which he kept in his pocket. Weirdly, it seemed to be working again, at least most of the time, as was his Juicy Juicy. Trevor figured this was because everyone around him still had free will, since only he had been hit by a free will bomb.

"My luck is about to change!" said Trevor, who randomly looked down and saw a shiny silver dollar lying on the ground. "Sweet!" said Trevor, as he put the silver dollar in his pocket.

"Hey, Alex," yelled Trevor. Alex climbed out of the tree in his front yard and ran over to Trevor. "Want to have some fun?"

"Yeah, man," said Alex. "What do you want to do?" Alex was a good friend.

"Let's do something exciting!" said Trevor.

"Okay," said Alex, "like what?"

"Follow me," said Trevor, who began walking back toward his minivan. When they got to the usual spot around the corner, Trevor pushed the button on his remote control, causing his minivan time machine to appear. Alex didn't understand what he saw.

"That's weird," said Alex, "I could have sworn there wasn't a car here. It's like this minivan just appeared out of thin air." Trevor pushed the button again, causing the minivan to disappear.

"Whoa, what's going on here?" yelled Alex. Trevor smiled and pushed the button again, causing the minivan to reappear.

"Get in," said Trevor. "There's something I want to show you."

Chapter 121: Road Trip

Trevor put the car in gear and started driving out of the neighborhood. "What are you doing?" said Alex. "You can't drive a minivan! You're only ten!"

Trevor realized he was being controlled by the Murkians but didn't care. He always wanted to drive a car.

"Relax," said Trevor, "I promise nothing bad will happen." Trevor knew that was a lie since he had no idea what might happen. Still, he was enjoying himself.

"Jeeves," said Trevor, "teach me how to drive a car."

Alex's eyes widened when he heard Jeeves, the onboard computer, reply. "Okay, whatever you like, sir." Alex didn't say anything, but instead listened in stunned silence.

"Stop at the stop sign ahead," said Jeeves. Trevor followed the instructions. Alex thought about jumping out of the car but didn't because he wanted to see what would happen next.

"Now put the car in park and adjust your mirrors," said Jeeves. Jeeves then explained how to set the car mirrors so that Trevor could see the cars behind him on the road, without a blind spot. The trick was to set the left mirror out to the left a fair bit, so that cars passing on the left went from the middle mirror, to the left mirror, and then to Trevor's side vision without any gaps.

"Most people do not set their left mirror correctly," said Jeeves, "which is why most cars have a blind spot behind them on the left, and sometimes on the right too. This can lead to accidents, so be very careful when passing other cars. In many cases, they can't see you."

"In fact," continued Jeeves, "it's best not to pass cars any more than necessary. If you have your mirrors set correctly, it's usually safer to get in the right lane and let the other cars pass you when you are driving on the freeway." Trevor put the car in gear and drove off.

"On the freeway!" yelled Alex. Alex started to regret not jumping out of the car when he had the chance.

"Trust me!" said Trevor. "We're fine. Let's live a little!" Trevor worked his way down some smaller streets, turned onto the entrance ramp, and then merged onto the freeway.

"Keep your eyes forward, except to check your mirrors," explained Jeeves. "Don't look at your friends or try to use a phone while you drive. People die in car accidents that way all the time."

"Also, keep a good following distance behind the car in front of you," said Jeeves. "Just ask yourself how close you would want to be to the car in front of you if it slammed on its breaks or was in an accident. You need to give yourself enough of a gap that you can avoid hitting the other cars, no matter what happens. The farther back you are, the better."

Trevor remembered his dad explaining the "two seconds rule" to him, which meant passing a point on the ground at least two seconds after the car in front of him. That didn't seem like much time to react to something bad to Trevor, so he followed even farther behind.

"Jeeves, give me directions to the nearest high stakes poker game," said Trevor. "I want to make some money." Trevor started to get excited.

"Are you crazy?" asked Alex. "We don't even have any money!"

"I've got a shiny silver dollar," said Trevor, "and I can read people like a book."

"Take the next exit," said Jeeves. "There's an illegal card game fifteen miles from here."

Chapter 122: High Stakes Poker

Trevor and Alex drove out into the country to a huge shed that had hundreds of cars parked all around it. "Here we are," said Jeeves. "Just be careful. Illegal poker games attract dangerous people. Some of the gamblers carry guns and knives to protect themselves from thieves and cheaters who carry guns and knives. You kids really shouldn't be going in there."

"Whatever!" said Trevor, who was still being controlled by the Murkians. "Come on, Alex, I'm sure we'll be fine."

Alex followed Trevor into the huge shed which was filled with dozens of poker tables, each with gamblers crowding around them. They walked over to a scary looking man who looked like he was in charge.

"I'd like to play some poker," said Trevor. The scary looking man didn't see Trevor at first.

Trevor repeated himself. "I'd like to play some poker," said Trevor again. The man looked down at Trevor.

"Go find your daddy," said the man, as he laughed. "This game is for grownups!"

Trevor was wearing his pajamas, so he wasn't afraid of anything. "Either let me play, or I'm going to call the cops and have everyone here arrested," said Trevor. This got the scary looking man's attention.

"Listen here, you little punk," said the man, "nobody threatens me!" The man tried pushing Trevor out of the shed, not realizing it was impossible. Using his pajamas, Trevor grabbed the man's hand and twisted it, causing the scary looking man to fall to one knee."

"Ow! Ow! Ow!" said the scary looking man in disbelief. His mind couldn't process being manhandled by a fifth grader. "Okay, you've got to be the youngest looking eighteen year old I've ever seen," said the man. "I'll get you a table right away."

Alex was having a great time. "That was awesome!" said Alex. "How did you do that?"

"Karate lessons," said Trevor. "Now sit back and watch me play some poker!"

Trevor started at the small stakes table where the minimum bet was one dollar. Using his Juicy Juicy and mind reading skills, Trevor knew exactly which cards everyone else had in their hands, and where the other cards were in the deck. Trevor entered the game when he knew he would probably win his first hand and won five dollars. He put his lucky silver dollar back into his pocket for safe keeping. Then he only bet more money when he knew he was going to win. Within thirty minutes, Trevor had one hundred dollars.

"That was some great poker playing!" said Alex.

"I'm just getting started," said Trevor. "Let's find some higher stakes tables."

Trevor then cleaned up at the five dollar minimum bet table and won five hundred dollars. At the twenty dollar minimum bet table, Trevor won two thousand dollars. At the hundred dollar minimum bet table, Trevor raked in even more money.

"How much money do you have?" asked Alex, who couldn't believe what was happening.

"About ten thousand dollars," said Trevor.

"Awesome!" said Alex. "Let's go home. We can buy a lot of Legos with that money!"

"True," said Trevor, who loved Legos, especially Star Wars Legos. "But I'm not ready to go home just yet. I want to play in the Big Game."

"The Big Game?" asked Alex. "What's that?"

Chapter 123: The Big Game

The Big Game was the main attraction at the center of the shed. Seven players were playing when Trevor and Alex walked up. Dozens of other people crowded around the table to see what was going on.

"Deal me in," said Trevor, as he plopped his money pile on the table. Even though Trevor had more than ten thousand dollars, he still had less money than everyone else at the table. Everyone else at the table started laughing.

"Where did you get all of that money, kid?" asked the dealer, as he glanced over at the man in charge. The man in charge nodded back, signaling the dealer to let Trevor play.

The Big Game had five very wealthy individuals playing in it and two professional poker players. The professional poker players were winning lots of money. They called the rich players "whales," behind their back. The whales were losing money, but kept playing anyway.

"Hi, I'm Big Jim," said one of the professional poker players. Big Jim liked to talk to the other players, hoping that they would give something away about their cards by how they talked back.

"Hello," said Trevor calmly, as he shoved all his money into the middle of the table. "I raise you everything I've got." Everyone called Trevor, including Big Jim, by betting as much as Trevor had, only to find out that Trevor had the best hand. This happened over and over again.

"How come you never lose?" asked Big Jim, who was getting upset. He didn't like losing.

Trevor didn't reply, but just kept playing. Within an hour, Trevor had one hundred thousand dollars. Every time Trevor won a hand, the whole room clapped, amazed at what they saw.

"Seriously," said Big Jim, "I've never seen someone be so darn lucky!" Big Jim, who made his living playing poker, was not happy for Trevor. He was going to have to sell his truck if he lost any more money. He continued to grumble to himself as they played more poker.

"It's like you know what cards are going to be dealt, before they're dealt!" said Big Jim. Trevor didn't say anything back. "Do you hear what I'm saying, kid?" said Big Jim. "I'm saying you're a no good cheater!"

Trevor leaned back in his chair. "I am not a cheater!" said Trevor, though he realized that wasn't exactly true. The Murkians had really got him into a tricky situation.

"Let's just go home," said Alex to Trevor. "You've got over two hundred thousand dollars."

"Okay," said Trevor, who could tell that Big Jim was the kind of guy who was dangerous when he got mad. "Let's go."

Trevor folded his hand and started stacking up his money. As he did, Big Jim glared at him. "I want my money back!" said Big Jim. "Nobody cheats Big Jim and gets away with it!"

As Trevor and Alex left the building and walked over to their car, they saw that Big Jim was following them into the parking lot. "Hold it right there!" said Big Jim. "Give me my money right now, or there's going to be trouble." Big Jim pulled out a knife and pointed it at Trevor.

"Get in the car," said Trevor to Alex. Alex did just that, locking the door behind him.

"I figure half of your money is mine," said Big Jim, "but I'm going to take it all, one way or the other. That's what you get for being a cheater!"

"I see your point," said Trevor, "but you shouldn't ever pull a knife on a kid. That's not very nice." Trevor shot Big Jim with a wormhole from the homologizer in his watch. Big Jim was gone.

Chapter 124: Charitable Donation

Alex saw Trevor shoot Big Jim with a wormhole and couldn't believe his eyes. Alex was even more surprised when he saw Big Jim walk out of another wormhole, one second later. The new Big Jim wore a coat and a tie, carried a briefcase, had shaved off his beard and mustache, and had a new haircut. He looked like a new man.

"Where am I?" asked Big Jim, who looked at Trevor. Alex was still in the car watching.

"You're at the poker game," said Trevor. "Are you all right?"

"Yes," said Big Jim, "but I had the weirdest dream just now." He scratched his head. "It had something to do with you," said Big Jim, who was looking at Trevor. "Can I talk to you about it?" Trevor nodded his head yes. The two of them sat down on a picnic table next to the parking lot.

"I've spent most of my life playing poker," said Big Jim, "and I've always been good at it. That's how I've made my living since I was a kid." He paused. "But now I realize I've been wasting my life. How am I making the world a better place by playing poker?" He paused again. "I'm not," he admitted to himself. "Tricking people out of their money is exploiting human weaknesses. I feel ashamed for what I've done, and for all of the people I've hurt."

Trevor was impressed with Big Jim. He was also impressed with the Fruit Smoothians, who really knew how to bring out the best in a person.

"So I've decided," continued Big Jim, "to dedicate the rest of my life to helping people who have gambling problems." Big Jim started to tear up. "Did you know that I've taken people's cars from them? I always laughed at them before. Now I feel sorry for them, and their families. I bet I've caused families to get kicked out of their homes, too. I feel so ashamed."

"Well, it sounds like you are going to start doing the right thing," said Trevor, who was feeling ashamed of himself as well. Trevor didn't feel good about using his Juicy Juicy and mind reading skills to win at poker. Even though Trevor had followed the rules, it felt like cheating to him. Trevor didn't like feeling like a cheater, or tricking people out of their money.

"I'm going to go back into that shed," said Big Jim, "and see how many people I can help. I'm going to find people with gambling problems and help them stop. I'm going to use my own money, which I won from gambling, to help pay some of their bills, and to make their lives better." He paused again. "Then I'm going to find a real job, a job that helps people."

"You're great at math," said Trevor. "Why don't you become a high school math teacher?"

Big Jim lit up. "That's a great idea!" he said. "By the way, I've got something for you." Big Jim pulled a wand and a photograph out of his briefcase and gave them to Trevor. "I have no idea how I got these two things, but I know they belong to you," said Big Jim.

The back of the photograph had a note on it explaining how to use the memory wand to erase people's memories, as needed. The photograph was of Rainbow, with a tear coming down her cheek. "Dang it!" thought Trevor to himself. He knew what he had to do.

"Here's two hundred thousand dollars," said Trevor to Big Jim. "Half of it is yours anyway. Use it to get your teaching degree. The other half you can use to help people, especially those with gambling problems."

"Really?" said Big Jim, who was overwhelmed. "Thank you! Thank you!" Big Jim got up and gave Trevor a big hug. "I won't let you down! I'm going to be the best teacher ever, and I can't wait to start helping people. If you ever need anything - anything at all - just let me know!"

Chapter 125: The Carnivorous Predator

Trevor got back into the car and explained everything to Alex. He told Alex about the time machine, the Fruit Smoothians, being a secret agent, and the Murkian threat. Alex took it very well.

"I'm being controlled by the Murkians right now," said Trevor, "but they can't make me do anything I wouldn't do on my worst day. I think they wanted to make me rich to try to convince me to stay here, in my reality, and not try to save the Fruit Smoothians, ten thousand years in the future. Of course, they would have liked it even better if Big Jim had killed me."

Alex kept on nodding, as he had all along, pretending to believe everything that Trevor said. Finally, he said something. "Yeah, Trevor, you realize that what you are saying is ridiculous, right? I mean, making a car disappear is a pretty cool trick, and I don't know what happened to Big Jim exactly, but this minivan is not a time machine. It's a regular minivan, just like my mom's."

Trevor smiled. "Buckle up, Alex. We're taking this time machine for a spin." Trevor put on his seatbelt too. "Jeeves, can you take us to see some dinosaurs?" Jeeves said that he could.

"My parents have a phone service built into their car too," laughed Alex. "That doesn't make your minivan a time machine."

Suddenly the minivan's powerful engine, more powerful than the Sun, came on line, purring with its unmistakable sound. "That's different," said Alex. Then the car lifted off the ground gracefully and hovered several hundred feet in the air. "And that's different too!"

The time machine then started going back in time, around 67 million years. The billions of days and nights that the time machine passed through caused the light to flicker outside like a fluorescent light bulb, until the flickering became so great that the light outside was constant but dimmed. The landscape changed beneath their time machine rapidly due to erosion and continental drift, at one point becoming an ocean, and then land again. When the time travel stopped, the minivan time machine hovered over a vast forest, one hundred feet in the air. In a clearing there were some plant eating dinosaurs drinking out of a pond.

Suddenly, all of the dinosaurs started to run, as if scared for their lives. A tyrannosaurus rex, twenty feet tall and forty feet long, came running out of the forest, looking for a smaller dinosaur to eat. All of the other dinosaurs, who were smaller and could run faster, got away.

"Let's go down there and check things out," said Trevor to Alex. Alex looked at him like he was crazy. The tyrannosaurus rex looked up at the time machine for a second, and then ignored it like it would a bird.

"Jeeves, drop down to eye level with the tyrannosaurus rex, getting as close as you can without letting him touch us," said Trevor, who was being controlled by the Murkians. Trevor realized they would love it if Trevor were eaten by a dinosaur, but knew he was perfectly safe in his reinforced time machine, so strong it could pass through a star.

Trevor and Alex were face to face with the carnivorous predator, who stared directly at them. The tyrannosaurus rex snapped his jaws at the time machine and barely missed, as Jeeves backed up just in time. The dinosaur started to run at the time machine. Jeeves backed up faster and faster. "Get us out of here!" yelled Alex.

Chapter 126: The Destruction of the Earth

Jeeves pulled up just in time, narrowly avoiding the tyrannosaurus rex, and hovered one hundred feet in the air. Several flying dinosaurs with wingspans of thirty feet flew by.

"Whoa!" said Trevor. "Those flying dinosaurs must be five hundred pounds each!"

"Is this safe?" asked Alex. "I mean, you're being controlled by the Murkians, right?"

"True," said Trevor. "I tell you what – you're in charge now. Whatever you say, we'll do."

This made Alex feel better. "Okay, sounds good." He breathed a sigh of relief. "Jeeves," said Alex, "what should we look at next?"

"Well, there's going to be a huge asteroid that hits the planet Earth in a couple of million years. The impact will be so large that a dust cloud will cover the sky, blotting out the Sun for a year. Most of the plants will die, as will most of the animals that feed on the plants, including all of the dinosaurs, except for some birds. We can watch from a safe distance, if you like."

"Can we watch from outer space?" asked Alex. Jeeves followed Alex's request and positioned the time machine in outer space, but close enough for a good view. Trevor and Alex saw an asteroid approaching at tremendous speed, heading straight for the Earth.

"That asteroid is eight miles wide," said Jeeves. "When it hits the Earth, the impact will be greater than a billion atomic bombs going off, all at once."

Trevor and Alex started thinking about the seriousness of what they were seeing. Most of the life forms on the planet were about to die. Some day in the future, another massive asteroid might hit the Earth, and kill most of the life on the planet again.

"Wait a second!" said Trevor. "What if I shoot the asteroid with a wormhole and send it into the Sun? I could prevent this calamity from happening!" Trevor started asking Jeeves to maneuver the time machine to get into position.

"Wait a second," said Alex. "We shouldn't be changing history like this, should we?"

Trevor remembered his agreement to do whatever Alex said, and so listened closely.

"Actually," said Jeeves, "there is considerable evidence that this asteroid changes the evolutionary path of most of the animals on the planet Earth. In fact," he continued, "humans might not have ever evolved without this asteroid."

"Really?" said Trevor.

"Absolutely," said Jeeves. "The extinction of the dinosaurs, as well as many other animals, made it possible for smaller animals to thrive, without having to worry about a tyrannosaurus rex or another dinosaur eating them all of the time. Since humans evolved from these smaller animals, in some sense we owe our existence to this asteroid."

The asteroid passed right by the time machine and hit the planet Earth, creating an impact area one hundred miles wide. The heat from the blast seemed to catch the atmosphere of the Earth around the impact on fire, and huge tsunami waves in the oceans wreaked devastation. A dust cloud began filling the skies, until the entire planet seemed to be covered in a dark blanket.

"Well, that's not something you see every day," said Alex.

Trevor was in shock. "We just witnessed the destruction of the Earth. I can't believe anything survived that impact, but I know something did. Life really is amazing."

"And that wasn't even the largest object to hit the Earth!" said Jeeves.

Chapter 130: The Creation of the Moon

"What was the largest object to hit the Earth?" asked Alex.

"Four and a half billion years ago, another planet about the size of Mars collided with the Earth," said Jeeves. "The collision was so great that it turned the surface of the Earth molten again and sent dirt, rock, and other debris into orbit around the Earth, which eventually came together to form the Moon." Trevor and Alex nodded their heads with wide-eyed amazement.

Suddenly, twenty Murkian starships wormholed into the space surrounding Trevor's time machine. They opened fire on Trevor and Alex, shooting lasers and torpedoes at them. Jeeves maneuvered to avoid some of the torpedoes. Others hit, but did no damage. Professor Spark's reinforced outer shell on the time machine held strong.

"Where are those Fruit Smoothian battle cruisers?" asked Trevor. "They're supposed to be protecting the Earth!"

"They are," said Jeeves, "back in your home reality. They didn't know you'd be going back in time, so they aren't here right now." Trevor realized that the Murkians had tricked him again.

The Murkians started talking to Trevor and Alex through the car radio. "Surrender to us now, and we'll spare the planet Earth. There's no reason we need to be enemies."

"They've got a lot of nerve," said Trevor to Alex. "They just tried to kill us, and now they're saying they want to be friends. What a bunch of liars!"

Alex tapped Trevor on the shoulder. "Trevor," said Alex, "I think they can hear you. Look!"

All twenty of the Murkian ships fired wormholes at their time machine. Trevor realized that those wormholes could send them anywhere. Trevor didn't want them to end up in a Murkian prison, never to be seen again.

Trevor focused his mind on the wormholes, causing all of them to miss his time machine, though just barely. The wormholes circled around for another pass to try to hit Trevor's time machine. As they approached, Trevor raised his hands as if to grab the wormholes. He then closed his eyes and took a deep breath. For the first time, Trevor felt like he could sense the wormholes, as well as the rest of the universe. All of the wormholes stopped, obeying Trevor's every command.

Next, Trevor started moving the wormholes in a juggling pattern, weaving them all around in the sky. The Murkian ships, aware that they had lost control of their wormholes, started to back away. Trevor fired one wormhole at each ship. Each wormhole went around one Murkian ship and then shrank down to nothing. All of the Murkian ships were gone.

"Whoa!" said Alex. "How did you do that?"

"I don't know," said Trevor. "That was the first time I ever controlled so many wormholes, or someone else's wormhole, for that matter."

"Where did you send them?" asked Alex.

"I think those wormholes were set to send their targets to a Murkian prison of some sort," said Trevor. "That's probably where they went."

"Well, let's get out of here, before they return," said Alex.

"Good idea!" said Trevor.

Chapter 131: A New Strategy

Trevor and Alex returned to their home reality, one minute after they had driven off. When Trevor and Alex got out of the minivan, they could see the earlier version of themselves down the street, stopped at a stop sign, adjusting their mirrors. The earlier minivan then drove off around a corner.

Trevor pushed the button on his remote control, causing it to disappear. "That was the most fun ever!" said Alex. "But I sure am worried about those Murkians!"

"Not anymore," said Trevor, as he used his memory wand to erase Alex's memories of what they had just seen and done together. A bright light flashed from the end of the wand. Trevor felt bad about this, but realized it was for the greater good.

"Let's go play some basketball!" said Alex. Trevor agreed. They played outside for the rest of the day, and much of the next day, since it was the weekend.

At 4 p.m. on Sunday, Trevor picked up Farrah from her reality on his way back to Fruit Smoothie, returning one second after they had left. As they got out of the minivan, Professor Sparks, Banana Splash, Master Wraps, and Rainbow were anxiously standing there, waiting.

"What happened?" asked Professor Sparks. "Was Rainbow right? Did you figure out a new strategy for dealing with the Murkians?"

"No," said Trevor. Trevor and Farrah then brought everyone up to speed about their days back home. Farrah had stayed home, playing with her wormhole jump rope, but not traveling very far in time. Everyone was even more fascinated by Trevor's story, especially with the gambling, the dinosaurs, the Murkian attack, and Trevor's new abilities. The group went back inside District Headquarters, hoping to find a new strategy.

"Where did you say you got that shiny silver dollar?" asked Rainbow.

"I found it on the ground, half way between my time machine and my house," said Trevor, as he pulled it out of his pocket. "It's my lucky silver dollar."

"Lucky for whom?" said Professor Sparks. "Without that dollar, you wouldn't have had any money to gamble. Kind of a coincidence that you'd find a silver dollar like that, don't you think?"

"If I were the Murkians," said Master Wraps, "I'd put a tracking device in that silver dollar. Then I would always know where you were."

"Which explains how they knew where I was when they attacked me!" said Trevor. He was impressed by the cleverness of the Murkians' evil plans.

"We'll get that silver dollar to our scientists right away," said Banana Splash.

"And we do have a new strategy for dealing with the Murkians," announced Trevor solemnly. "I'm going to turn myself over to them."

Chapter 132: Ready for Action

"What?" yelled Farrah. "That's crazy. They'll kill you for sure."

Everyone looked at Trevor, puzzled by his plan to turn himself over to the Murkians. Only Rainbow wanted to hear more. "Let Trevor explain," she said.

"The Murkians have already attacked me twice," said Trevor. "Both times someone I cared about could have been hurt, or maybe many people. I don't want to take that chance anymore."

"That's the stupidest thing I've ever heard," said Farrah. "Rainbow, tell him that this is the Murkians controlling him."

Trevor continued, "But it will all be a trick. Once I'm captured, the rest of you can track me using my lucky silver dollar. After I figure out how the Murkians are controlling us, I'll give the signal, and the Fruit Smoothian defense forces can come to my rescue and defeat the Murkians."

"What a silly idea," said Professor Sparks.

"I don't like it either," said Master Wraps. Banana and Farrah shook their heads and laughed as well. Only Rainbow wanted to discuss the idea more.

"It's risky," said Rainbow, "but Trevor's plan has merit. You should think his idea through very carefully."

"What for?" said Banana. "It's crazy! Trevor's our key asset. We shouldn't just turn him over to the enemy!"

"On the other hand," said Farrah, "the last time we all hated an idea this much, it was the Murkians controlling us. Maybe Trevor's idea is brilliant, but we just aren't giving it a chance."

"Okay," said Banana.

The group spent the next hour discussing the plan, gradually liking it more and more. Each person contributed an idea, until finally they had a plan that everyone liked.

"It's bold, audacious, and clever," said Master Wraps. "If this works, it will go down in history as one of the greatest military achievements ever. The fate of the galaxy depends on it."

"One thing we have going for us," said Rainbow, "is that there is a 50% chance that Trevor will save us all. In other words, we have plenty of reason for hope."

"Yeah, but what about that other 50%?" said Professor Sparks. "We have no idea what horrible fate might await us – not to mention the rest of the galaxy. If Trevor fails, the galaxy could be doomed to billions of years of slavery." Everyone looked at the professor, who quickly realized he shouldn't have said that.

"Visualize accomplishing your goal," interrupted Rainbow. "Think how great it will be when we defeat the Murkians. Think about your training and how hard you've worked to get to this point. Stay positive and optimistic, and believe in yourself. You can accomplish anything."

"That's what I meant to say," said the professor meekly, looking down with a smile.

Trevor began visualizing how great it would be to be free of the Murkians. "Trevor," said Rainbow, "what do you think?"

"Let's do it," said Trevor, "I'm ready for action."

Chapter 133: Murkos

After a good night's sleep, everyone met back at District Headquarters the next morning to prepare for Trevor turning himself over to the Murkians. Trevor insisted that he go by himself, just in case things went bad. "There's no reason for anyone else to risk getting hurt too," he said.

"That makes sense," said Rainbow, "but be careful. You're the galaxy's best hope."

"Here's your lucky silver dollar back," said Banana. "The Murkians will be tracking you with it, which will make it easy for them to find you. What they don't know is that we'll be tracking you with it too."

"Also," said Rainbow, "I'll be with you every step of the way, reading your mind, and talking to you inside your head. When you're ready for the Murkian forces to converge on your position, just let me know."

"We've got most of our defense forces on standby," said Master Wraps. "As soon as Rainbow gives the signal, we'll be ready to do whatever you need."

"We'll all be waiting to get in the game," said Farrah. "I want to fight bad guys too."

"Me too," said Professor Sparks. "Jeeves and I are ready to help, however we can."

Everyone looked at Trevor, admiring his courage, and smothered him with a big group hug. "We love you," everyone said to Trevor.

"Okay, let's do this," said Trevor. "I'm as ready as I'll ever be."

With that, Rainbow opened a wormhole portal for Trevor. "Murkos is on the other side," said Rainbow. "Once you step through, they should arrest you within minutes."

Trevor stepped through the portal and waved goodbye to everyone as the portal closed down to nothing and disappeared. He was now on the planet Murkos. He looked around at a barren landscape of deserts and mountains. Sand and dust blew in his face. "It's hard to believe anyone lives here," thought Trevor to himself.

Trevor turned around and saw a dust storm in the distance heading straight for him. The dust storm looked like a wall of dirt one thousand feet high and many miles wide. Trevor looked around for cover and started to get very worried.

"Stay calm," said Rainbow inside Trevor's mind. "I can create a wormhole for you to come home at any time. Be patient for now."

Sure enough, a small Murkian patrol ship appeared on the horizon, coming toward Trevor very quickly. Trevor raised his hands to indicate his cooperation. The Murkian ship fired a wormhole at Trevor, which Trevor didn't resist. The wormhole went around Trevor, and then closed up. Trevor was gone.

Chapter 134: Khanos the Destroyer

"Where am I?" thought Trevor to himself. Trevor saw that he was in a large prison cell of some kind. Dozens of Murkians surrounded his prison cell, looking at him through the bars. Most of them were around five feet tall.

"This is Trevor the Time Traveler?" asked one of the Murkians. "But he's so small."

A larger Murkian, nearly six feet tall, zapped the Murkian who spoke with some kind of electricity gun, causing him to fall to the ground, writhing in pain. "Show our guest some respect." The other Murkians stepped back, making way for the tall Murkian to approach the prison cell.

"My name is Khanos the Destroyer," said the tall Murkian, who was clearly in charge. He was dressed like a general. "Welcome to our headquarters, deep underground on the planet Murkos."

Trevor couldn't believe his good luck. Five minutes into his mission and he had already located the enemy's headquarters. "Hello," said Trevor.

Khanos the Destroyer flipped a coin. He seemed disappointed with the result. Then he flipped the coin again. This time he seemed pleased with the result. He pulled out a large gun, pointed it at Trevor, and fired.

Trevor fell to the ground, shaken but not hurt. "Hey, stop that!" said Trevor. "That tickled!" Trevor's pajamas had protected him from certain death.

"That's what I thought," said Khanos, pausing for a moment. "You see, I have a problem. We all know there's a 50% chance that you will save your galaxy, right?"

"Yes," said Trevor.

"So that means there's no way for me to kill you," he continued, "with 100% certainty. But I want to kill you so badly," said Khanos. "You see my problem?"

Trevor marveled at the cruelness of this guy. "What was the coin all about?" asked Trevor.

"Well, I was trying to kill you with 50% probability," said Khanos. "I told myself I would only kill you if the coin came up heads. But it came up tails the first time, so I had to flip again." Trevor was thankful that Khanos didn't seem to understand probabilities very well.

"Well, those are the breaks," said Trevor. "You can't kill me with 50% probability if you are just going to keep flipping until you get what you want. That would be trying to kill me with 100% probability." Trevor couldn't believe he was explaining probabilities to the guy trying to kill him, but then remembered he was still being controlled by the Murkians.

Khanos smiled. "I like you," he said. "I still want to kill you, but I like you."

Trevor smiled back as he thought to Rainbow. "Send in the troops, Rainbow. I'm at the enemy's headquarters now!"

Chapter 135: Game Theory

Khanos flipped a switch on the wall, causing a buzzing sound to fill Trevor's head. Trevor suddenly had a hard time listening to his own thoughts. He realized that Rainbow wouldn't be able to read his mind any more.

"And I really like your plan, too!" said Khanos. "First, you surrender yourself, hoping we take you to our headquarters. Well, here we are!"

Trevor was shocked and disturbed. Khanos seemed to know their plan all too well.

"Now that you've called in the Fruit Smoothian troops, they can destroy our headquarters, with you in it. If I can't kill you, maybe they can."

"They would never kill me," countered Trevor.

"Never?" asked Khanos, who laughed. "I almost got them to destroy an entire galaxy. I think I can get them to destroy Murkian headquarters. All I have to do is make them think you are no longer here, which will be easy enough. After all, I control all of them."

Trevor feared that Khanos was right. He was in real danger and had no way to communicate with any of his friends.

"The best part," said Khanos, who was laughing again, "is that after the Fruit Smoothians destroy Murkian headquarters, I'm going to let them think that they have their free will back. I'll give them just enough free will that their Juicy Juicy will work again, at least enough to convince them that they've won the war. Of course, I'll still be controlling them from time to time, when it counts. With their advanced technology, they'll be able to take over the Milky Way galaxy better than anyone. Once they do, I'll step in as ruler of both galaxies."

"Why are you doing this?" asked Trevor. "What is the point of all of this?"

"Game theory," said Khanos. "You see, the Andromeda and Milky Way galaxies are on a collision course and will combine into one bigger galaxy in four billion years." Trevor remembered seeing the two galaxies merge with Professor Sparks on his first trip in the time machine.

"This means that our peace treaty, where we each stay in separate galaxies, can't last forever," continued Khanos. "Eventually this would have become painfully obvious to both sides. It's basic game theory."

Trevor had heard enough. He reached for his homologizer and fired. As he did, he could see that Khanos was amused. "Oh, I'm sorry," said Khanos, "does your homologizer not work? What unfortunate timing!" Trevor tried his walkie talkie, but it didn't work either.

Just then, the room began to shake. "Great," said Khanos. "I see the Fruit Smoothians have begun their attack. Good luck to you all!" Khanos created a wormhole with his hand, and then stepped though. "Good bye!"

157

Chapter 136: Switch Flip

Trevor took the silver dollar tracking device out of his pocket and tossed it through Khanos's wormhole, just as it was disappearing. "Brilliant!" he thought to himself. Trevor then tried to communicate to Rainbow, but couldn't because of the buzzing sound in his head.

"Quick, flip that switch on the wall," said Trevor to the Murkians, "or we're all going to die."

The Murkian soldiers didn't budge. "We have orders," said one soldier. "It will be an honor to die for our people." Trevor felt the same way, but didn't want to die just yet. He had work to do.

"But you're being controlled by free will bombs," said Trevor. "Try to snap out of it." Trevor didn't make any progress with his captors. Another bomb went off, knocking everyone to the ground. Trevor realized he had only seconds before the entire underground building was destroyed.

Trevor remembered his advanced training with Banana and his discussions about the curvature of spacetime with Professor Sparks. He stood up, sensing space and time, as he had at least once before. He focused on trying to stop time, like Banana could, but was unsuccessful.

Trevor's head was still filled with the buzzing sound. "Stop it!" thought Trevor, as he looked sharply at the switch. Amazingly, the switch flipped as if obeying Trevor's command, and the buzzing sound went away.

"Stop the attack! Stop the attack!" thought Trevor to Rainbow.

Everything became very quiet. A wormhole opened up next to Trevor. Trevor could see Rainbow through the wormhole on the other side. Trevor walked through the wormhole which closed up behind him. He was surprised to find himself reunited with everyone on a Fruit Smoothian battle cruiser.

"Trevor!" yelled everyone, who smothered him in another big group hug. "We lost contact with your tracking device, so we thought you must be somewhere else," said Master Wraps. "Sorry for almost killing you!"

"Not to worry," said Trevor. "I threw the tracking device through the wormhole that the Murkian leader Khanos used to escape. If we hurry, we can use it to find him."

Chapter 140: A Moon in the Middle of Nowhere

"I've picked up the signal," said Banana. "Khanos is deep underground, on a moon in the middle of nowhere, half way across the Andromeda galaxy. We never would have looked there!"

"All forces, converge on the coordinates provided by Agent Splash," said Master Wraps. The Fruit Smoothian battle cruisers wormholed to the moon and surrounded it. Hundreds of Fruit Smoothian soldiers then wormholed into Khanos' bunker in the moon.

"We've got him," said one of the soldiers, over the intercom.

"We better get down there quick," said Master Wraps. Rainbow opened up a wormhole that they all walked through. Khanos the Destroyer was in handcuffs, surrounded by Fruit Smoothian soldiers. He looked depressed and beaten. Trevor saw his lucky silver dollar on the floor. He picked it up and put it in his pocket, smiling at Khanos as he did.

"I still have a chance," said Khanos to Trevor. "The game's not over yet."

"Shoot him," said Master Wraps.

160

"No, you can't!" said Trevor. Master Wraps raised his hand, indicating to delay his order.

"Why not?" asked Master Wraps.

"First of all," said Trevor, "he's unarmed. Second, he may have valuable information. Third," continued Trevor, "if you want to shoot an unarmed man, then I have to think that he's not the one controlling you."

Rainbow was very impressed with Trevor's reasoning. After some more discussion, everyone else agreed too.

"Our scientists say that we are looking for devices, called detonators, which control each free will bomb," said Banana. "If we can destroy these devices, then we will get our free will back. Since thousands of free will bombs were detonated on Fruit Smoothie, we're probably looking for thousands of little devices."

Everyone turned and looked at Khanos. "Where are they?" yelled Master Wraps. Khanos looked away, trying not to answer, but glanced for an instant toward another room. Farrah ran into the room.

"I found them!" yelled Farrah. Everyone followed Farrah into the room, including Master Wraps who dragged the handcuffed Khanos into the room as well.

Boxes of thousands of small devices, each about the size of a mobile phone, were stacked up on one side of the room. "Are these the detonators?" asked Master Wraps to Khanos. Khanos, who was slumped over, didn't respond. "If we destroy these devices, will we get our free will back?"

"Yes," said Rainbow. "I've read Khanos's mind. These are the devices he was using to control you. If we destroy all of these devices, you will get your free will back."

Chapter 141: Heads

"I still have a chance," said Khanos to Trevor again. "You still haven't won."

"Wait," said Master Wraps to everyone. "What do you mean, Khanos? Tell us!" Khanos was happy to talk.

"I tried to kill Trevor over and over again," said Khanos. "I tried abducting him at his school, shooting him with twenty Murkian starships, and even shooting him myself. All of these attempts failed because of one simple reason: physics dictates that Trevor has precisely a 50% chance to save your galaxy, not more, not less." Everyone tried to follow Khanos's logic, which was strange but somehow made sense.

"In fact, if I'm being perfectly honest," said Khanos, "something drew me to Trevor, like our fates were intertwined. I don't know why, but this moment had to happen."

"But, for the same reason that I couldn't kill Trevor with 100% certainty," continued Khanos, "Trevor can't save your galaxy with 100% certainty either. No matter what you do, there is still a 50% chance that Trevor won't save your galaxy. I still have a chance!"

With that, Khanos punched one of his guards, and then another, as if he was about to escape. Master Wraps then grabbed him by the shirt and punched Khanos in the face, knocking him unconscious. "I was getting tired of that guy," said Master Wraps. Everyone clapped.

"Still," said Professor Sparks, "his logic makes sense, doesn't it, Rainbow?"

"It is a bit of a mystery," said Rainbow, "but a mystery that is about to be resolved, I think."

Master Wraps offered a Dematerializer gun to Trevor. "Fire away, young man," said Master Wraps, "you've earned it!"

"Hey, wait a second!" said Farrah. "Why does Trevor get to destroy the detonators? I found them!" Master Wraps rolled his eyes. He wasn't used to resolving disputes between siblings.

"Let's flip for it," said Trevor. "Heads I win, tails you win." Farrah nodded in agreement.

Trevor took his lucky silver dollar out of his pocket and flipped it into the air. Farrah held her breath as the coin rolled along the ground, and then gasped when she saw it was heads this time. "Dang it!" she said. Farrah was disappointed, but also happy for Trevor. Trevor took the Dematerializer gun from Master Wraps and shot the detonators, causing all of them to disappear.

"Ah," said Professor Sparks. "That's why Trevor had a 50% chance to save Fruit Smoothie. The other 50% chance was that Farrah would save Fruit Smoothie. We didn't know it, but it was their destiny, one or the other of them."

Everyone started cheering. "I have my Juicy Juicy back!" yelled one soldier, and then another, and then another. "Trevor saved us!" said another soldier.

"We all saved the galaxy!" yelled Trevor. "It was a team effort. None of us could have accomplished this without working together. Great work, everyone!"

"But why didn't we know there was a 50% chance that Farrah would save Fruit Smoothie?" asked Professor Sparks. No one seemed to hear him because of all of the cheering. The professor stared at Trevor's silver dollar, looking at it suspiciously.

Chapter 142: Our True Enemy

"Wait a second," said Banana Splash, "something's not right here. My Juicy Juicy indicates that someone here still doesn't have free will."

Khanos the Destroyer, who had been lying on the ground unconscious, having been hit by Master Wraps, started to wake up. "What happened?" he said.

"We won, that's what happened!" said one of the soldiers. Banana was not so sure.

"Where are the other detonators?" asked Banana. "Someone here still doesn't have free will."

"What?" said Khanos. "That's all of the detonators that I have."

"He's telling the truth," said Rainbow. "He doesn't know where the other detonators are."

"Who still doesn't have free will?" asked Professor Sparks.

Banana pulled out a brand new looking piece of equipment and started walking around the room. He ended up next to Khanos the Destroyer. "Everyone here has free will," said Banana, "except for Khanos. He is still being controlled by a free will bomb."

"That's ridiculous!" said Khanos. "No one would dare try to control me. I am the ruler of my galaxy. People fear me. I am Khanos the Destroyer!"

"That would explain how absurd this guy is," said Trevor. Farrah and Professor Sparks nodded in agreement. "I mean, who talks like that?"

"He kind of sounds like you," said Farrah, who was smiling at Master Wraps, "when you were being controlled at first!" Master Wraps blushed, realizing it was true.

"Well, maybe for a few minutes there," Master Wraps admitted. He thought for a moment. "Take him away," said Master Wraps, "but treat Khanos humanely. We may need his cooperation later."

"And be on the lookout for more bad guys, everyone," said Banana Splash. "At this point we have to assume that everyone in the Andromeda galaxy is being controlled by someone."

"And the scary part," said Professor Sparks, "is that we have no idea who it might be."

"We do know one thing," said Master Wraps. "Whoever is controlling the Andromeda galaxy almost took over the Milky Way galaxy as a bonus. We have to assume our true enemy will try again."

Chapter 143: Emergency Meeting

Trevor, Farrah, Professor Sparks, Banana Splash, Master Wraps, and Rainbow returned to Fruit Smoothie through one of Rainbow's wormholes. As they walked toward District Headquarters, they saw the planet bustling again. Everyone was smiling about having their Juicy Juicy back. Life was returning to normal.

"We can't thank you enough for saving our planet!" said Master Wraps.

Banana nodded in agreement. "Master Wraps and I live here, and it's our job to protect Fruit Smoothie. It's quite extraordinary the way the four of you risked your lives to save us. We will forever be in your debt. If you ever need anything - anything at all - just let us know."

Trevor thanked them back for protecting Earth and the rest of the Milky Way galaxy for billions of years. "Helping you was the least we could do," said Trevor. Everyone entered District Headquarters.

"What about all of the people in the Andromeda galaxy?" asked Farrah. "What will happen to them?"

"Well, our treaty with the Murkians is off, that's for sure," said Master Wraps. "Looking back, we made a mistake to ignore the evil in their galaxy, an evil that almost took over our galaxy as well. From now on, we're going to fight evil, wherever it exists, to whatever extent we can. We're going to start by trying to free everyone in the Andromeda galaxy."

Banana nodded. "It may take us years," said Banana, "but it's the right thing to do. Also, now we know that the security of the Milky Way galaxy depends on it. With our Juicy Juicy back and the Murkian leadership captured, we should be able to do a lot of good."

"Can I help?" asked Trevor. Farrah, Professor Sparks, and Rainbow wanted to help too.

Master Wraps thought for a moment. "When the time is right, we may call upon you again," he said. "But for now, we'd like you to go home and enjoy your normal lives. The Milky Way galaxy is safe for now. We should be able to handle things from here."

Everyone took the elevator down to B343. As the six of them exited the elevator, dozens of Fruit Smoothians working at their jobs stopped what they were doing and started cheering and clapping for their six heroes.

"Thank you, thank you," said Master Wraps. "But everyone get back to work. This is no time for us to let our guard down." Everyone followed his orders as the six of them entered a large conference room. Dozens of other secret agents filed into the room as well, including Sweet Chili and Hot Mustard who waved and smiled at them.

"While we're all very happy right now, we need to have one more emergency meeting," said Master Wraps. "It's standard procedure, really. We need to discuss what happened and to make sure we understand how to deal with future threats. Also, everything we say here will be recorded as a record of what happened."

Master Wraps then asked Trevor to say what happened after he surrendered to the Murkians. When Trevor got to the part about flipping the switch on the wall with his mind, Master Wraps got very excited, as did Banana.

"What are you saying?" asked Banana. "Are you saying you flipped a switch on the wall using only your mind? Nobody can do that!"

"Well, I can," said Trevor, "and on my worst day, too, when I was being controlled by a free will bomb. I can't wait to see what I can do on my best day!"

Chapter 144: The Fruit Smoothian Medal of Honor

"Banana," said Master Wraps, "I want you to keep meeting with Trevor and Farrah on a regular basis. Help them continue their training and teach them everything you know."

"I might learn a few things, too!" said Banana, who was still amazed at Trevor's ability to move things with his mind. Trevor and Farrah were excited to keep meeting with Banana.

"Trevor, Farrah, Professor Sparks, and Rainbow," said Master Wraps, "please come to the front of the room." They all got up and stood next to Master Wraps, facing everyone else in the room. "Because secrecy is one of our keys to success, we can't throw all of you a parade, or recognize you with a planet-wide fireworks display. However," he continued, "we can award the four of you our highest honor. In addition to making you honorary citizens of Fruit Smoothie, I am also awarding you the Fruit Smoothian Medal of Honor. Your bravery, heroism, and selfless dedication to the good of all people are inspirations for us all. Congratulations!" Master Wraps placed a beautiful medal around each of their necks.

Farrah smiled at Sweet Chili, who knew how much Farrah wanted a medal. Rainbow liked her medal too, which went well with her rainbow colors. "My friends back on Mystica are going to be so excited for me!" said Rainbow.

As Trevor received his second medal from the Fruit Smoothians, he tried very hard not to let it go to his head. "I did what any good person would do," said Trevor to Professor Sparks.

Professor Sparks smiled back at Trevor. "Yes, but people who are as good as you, even on their worst day, are hard to find." Professor Sparks gave Trevor a hug. "I couldn't be prouder to be your little brother!"

After the meeting, Trevor, Farrah, and Professor Sparks walked with Banana back to his house for some much deserved relaxation. Rainbow came with them too. Since everyone had their Juicy Juicy back, it was easy to find their way home through the arches.

"I already granted Farrah one wish," said Rainbow, "so I've decided to grant her brothers each one wish too." Rainbow smiled at Trevor and Professor Sparks who were both very excited. As they approached Banana's house, they saw their presents waiting for them by Banana's front door – a chicken and a wheelchair, presumably both of which could fly.

"Hey!" said Trevor, "That awesome! I always wanted a flying chicken!" Trevor's chicken flapped his wings and rose a few feet in the air before coming back to the ground.

"He understands everything you say," said Rainbow. "He'll make a great pet. I've already checked with Banana, who says he'll keep your flying chicken at his house for you."

The chicken let out a loud squawk. "I think I'll call him Squawky!" said Trevor. Everyone laughed. "Hey, where's Professor Sparks?"

Everyone looked around. "There he is!" yelled Farrah, who pointed in the sky at an old man flying around in a wheelchair.

Professor Sparks was clearly having a great time doing all kinds of fancy maneuvers in his flying wheelchair. He waved to everyone. "Woo hoo!"

Join the fun at
https://www.facebook.com/TrevorTheTimeTraveler about
Trevor's and Farrah's adventures, the science behind their stories,
and when the next Trevor the Time Traveler book is coming out.

Instead of dollars, the Fruit Smoothians use a currency which
loosely translates into English as a "Golden Thank You," the
official currency of the Milky Way Galaxy. The Fruit Smoothians
welcome you to use Golden Thank Yous too, both at home with
your parents and at school with your teachers. Learn more at
www.GoldenThankYous.com.

The front cover for this book was created using photos of the Andromeda galaxy (top, photo credit NASA/JPL-Caltech) and NGC 6744 (bottom, photo credit ESO) which is thought to look very similar to the Milky Way galaxy, our home.

The image of the Earth on the back cover of this book was created by NASA using many images collected by an orbiting satellite and then digitally projected onto a globe. The other image on the back (photo credit NASA/JPL-Caltech/JHUAPL/UCF) is a blurred version of an infrared photo of the Comet ISON taken by NASA's Spitzer Space Telescope on June 13, 2013.